Dear Reader,

Home, family, commu_____ values we cherish mos_____ ground us, comfort us, move us. They certainly provide the perfect inspiration around which to build a romance collection that will touch the heart.

And so we are thrilled to have the opportunity to introduce you to the Harlequin Heartwarming collection. Each of these special stories is a wholesome, heartfelt romance imbued with the traditional values so important to you. They are books you can share proudly with friends and family. And the authors featured in this collection are some of the most talented storytellers writing today, including favorites such as Brenda Novak, Janice Kay Johnson, Jillian Hart and Patricia Davids. We've selected these stories especially for you based on their overriding qualities of emotion and tenderness, and they center around your favorite themes–children, weddings, second chances, the reunion of families, the quest to find a true home and, of course, sweet romance.

So curl up in your favorite chair, relax and prepare for a heartwarming reading experience!

Sincerely,

The Editors

Janet Tronstad grew up on a farm in central Montana, spending many winter days reading books about the Old West and the gold rush days of Alaska. During college she got a chance to see the beauty of Alaska for herself when she worked a summer on Kodiak Island in a salmon factory, packing fish eggs for a Japanese firm. Janet now lives in Pasadena, California, where she writes full-time, when not dreaming of other places.

HARLEQUIN HEARTWARMING

Janet Tronstad

Seven Hundred Pansies

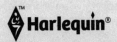

Harlequin®

TORONTO NEW YORK LONDON
AMSTERDAM PARIS SYDNEY HAMBURG
STOCKHOLM ATHENS TOKYO MILAN MADRID
PRAGUE WARSAW BUDAPEST AUCKLAND

Recycling programs
for this product may
not exist in your area.

ISBN-13: 978-0-373-36478-7

SEVEN HUNDRED PANSIES

Copyright © 2012 by Janet Tronstad

Originally published as A MATCH MADE IN DRY CREEK
Copyright © 2007 by Janet Tronstad

For questions and comments about the quality of this book
please contact us at Customer_eCare@Harlequin.ca

® and TM are trademarks of the publisher. Trademarks indicated with
® are registered in the United States Patent and Trademark Office, the
Canadian Trade Marks Office and in other countries.

www.Harlequin.com

Printed in U.S.A.

Seven Hundred Pansies

Dedicated with love to my younger sister, Doris, who shares her name with Mrs. Hargrove's daughter, but who is her own person. If there is any resemblance in character between my Doris and Mrs. Hargrove's daughter, other than the name and the faith they both share, it is coincidental. Of course, I have no objection if my Doris were to meet her Curt and have a happily ever after, but that will be her own story.

In addition, I'd like to acknowledge Norma Olsen, who lives on the farm down the road from my parents. She inspired this story with her many gifts of pansies to the women in the local church on Mother's Day.

CHAPTER ONE

WINTER AND GUILT didn't go well together in Dry Creek, Montana. Not even for Mrs. Hargrove, who, after decades of living in the small town, was used to the icy snow that sometimes trapped a person alone inside her house for days with only her own thoughts for company.

Mrs. Hargrove had lived her life with few regrets, so she generally spent the snowy days peacefully chopping vegetables for soup or putting together thousand-piece puzzles. This past winter she hadn't been able to do either of those things, however. Her conscience was troubling her, and she lacked the focus needed to figure out a puzzle or decide what to put into a pot of soup.

Instead, she sat and stared at the pictures on the mantel over her fireplace. There was the picture of her and her late husband, taken on their wedding day. And then there was a picture of her daughter, Doris June, taken when she graduated from high school. It wasn't a particularly good picture because, even though Doris June was smiling, she had a certain stiffness in her face that Mrs. Hargrove hadn't noticed until recently.

The graduation picture had been a last-minute idea and had been taken in a department store instead of at the high school like the pictures of the other students. Doris June hadn't seemed to care about a picture, but Mrs. Hargrove had wanted one even though, for years now, she had expected to exchange that graduation picture for a glowing picture of Doris June on her wedding day.

The wedding picture was going to be the real picture on the mantel place. It was what Mrs. Hargrove was waiting for.

But that wedding day never came. This winter, as she sat on her sofa looking at the picture she did have, Mrs. Hargrove finally accepted the truth. Doris June was not going to get married. The one huge miscalculation Mrs. Hargrove had made in her life had come back to haunt her and she couldn't stop fretting about it. She had unknowingly pushed away the only man Doris June had ever loved. For years, Mrs. Hargrove had hoped fate would take care of everything in time, but nothing had changed.

It had all come crashing back into Mrs. Hargrove's awareness in early January when she and Charley Nelson had sat down at her kitchen table to begin writing a history of their small town. The two of them were the oldest of the two hundred some residents of Dry Creek, and, when the state tourism board asked the town to write a section for an upcoming guidebook, everyone said she and Charley were the natural ones to write it. Both of them agreed to do the work, thinking it would be a good way for them to pass the cold winter months pleasantly.

It didn't take them long to realize what kind of trouble they were in, however. They knew it as soon as they opened the large white envelope the state tourism board had sent in care of the local café. Mrs. Hargrove and Charley had not known until then that the guidebook was being called *Stop at One-Stop-Sign Towns in Southern Montana.* Each town was supposed to begin their two pages of history and visitor attractions with an opening paragraph telling what made their particular old red stop sign unique.

It was a clever advertising idea and the state had invited several high schools in the area to help them with the tourism guide so the whole thing was a worthy project. Some art students were even going to take pictures of the signs and make a collage. Mrs. Hargrove and Charley were both one-hundred percent in favor of anything that helped students learn.

However, the stop sign in Dry Creek was the last thing either one of them wanted to write about.

Mrs. Hargrove wished people would just forget about that old sign.

Dry Creek's one stop sign was at the south end of town next to the Enger home place. Twenty-five years ago two local teenagers had hit the sign with an old blue pickup truck as they were beginning their elopement to Las Vegas. The passenger side of the truck had bent the signpost until it looked like the smashed half of a valentine. Both being responsible individuals, the teens had reported the damage to the sheriff, who then called their parents. From there, everything spun out of control until eventually the eloping couple were torn apart.

No one knew whether it was because of the broken-heart shape of the sign or the gossip about the two thwarted teens, but the story of the stop sign was told and retold until it became as close to a legend as anything Dry Creek had. A local musician even wrote a song about the heart sign and it played on the radio for a while so that people here and there throughout the state knew the story.

To this day, people would periodically place fresh flowers at the base of the rusted sign or carve their initials on the bent post. Every once in a while, there was talk of fixing the sign or even just pulling it down since the intersection it guarded was scarcely used any longer. But no one in an official capacity seemed able to make a decision to disturb the sign after its crooked form became part of the history of Dry Creek.

Charley had his elbows on Mrs. Hargrove's worn oak table and his right hand was curled around a cup of her fine brewed coffee. "You would have thought someone died when that sign was hit."

The contents of the envelope were sitting in front of him on the table. It was dusk and enough light was coming in the windows of Mrs. Hargrove's dining room that she hadn't turned on the overhead light yet.

"Sometimes a tragedy of the heart stays with people longer than a death," Mrs. Hargrove said after a moment or two. She didn't even notice that the light was fading. Her voice sounded tired to her own ears. "Look at Romeo and Juliet."

Charley grunted. "It was the parents in that one, too. Everybody always blames the parents for not understanding."

The two sat in silence as the room got a little darker.

Finally, Mrs. Hargrove said. "Well, we *understood*. We didn't approve, but we knew what was what. And at least we never tried to cover it up or anything. It was all out in the open. Everyone who was here twenty-five years ago knew it was Doris June and Curt who hit that sign. At least we've never denied anything."

Curt was Charley's son. He was the one driving the pickup when it hit the sign as he was eloping to Las Vegas with Doris June.

Mrs. Hargrove looked down at her coffee cup. "If things had turned out differently, the story of them and that sign would be a funny family story—just the kind of thing we'd laugh about as we bounced our grandbabies on our knees." Mrs. Hargrove stopped to sigh. She had no grandchildren. Still, she had a daughter who needed her. "As it is, I doubt either Curt or Doris June would like to see a reminder of that day in print anywhere and I'm not sure I have the stomach for it, either."

"If only they hadn't been so responsible and gone to the sheriff about the sign," Charley said. "We raised those kids to have values, and that's why it happened the way it did."

"Doris June always did tell the truth."

"Curt, too." Charley paused. "Of course, we couldn't let them get married once we knew what they were planning. Not at their ages."

Mrs. Hargrove lifted her cup of coffee and took a sip. "Who would think a little stop sign could change so many lives?"

Charley nodded. "It broke my son's heart."

Mrs. Hargrove looked up from her coffee cup at that. "It didn't break it so bad he didn't marry that New York woman the first chance he got."

"She wasn't from New York," Charley protested. "It was Chicago. And he didn't marry her until after he spent those four years in the army."

Mrs. Hargrove waved away the discrepancy. "All I know is she wasn't from here and she kept Curt away from here. He should have been here beside you run-

ning your farm all those years instead of
waiting until you decided to retire. Besides,
Doris June, at least, showed her affections
were sincere. She might have just turned
seventeen, but she always did understand
loyalty. She wasn't off marrying someone
else. Once she made up her mind, she kept
it made up."

"Some folks call that being inflexible."

"And some call it being solid and reli-
able."

"Well, whatever they call it, I didn't
notice you giving Doris June and Curt your
blessing on that day, either," Charley said.
"It wasn't only the Nelson family that was
up in arms."

Mrs. Hargrove nodded. He was right.
"What else could we do? Doris June had
just turned seventeen. I wanted her to go
to college and have a chance at the world.
You know I didn't object to Curt himself,
it was just the timing of things."

"Yeah, me, too. I loved Doris June like
the daughter I never had. But I thought I
was being a good parent. What did two

seventeen-year-old kids know about getting married?"

"They were just too young," Mrs. Hargrove said, and Charley nodded.

They spent the next five minutes drinking their coffee and trying to think of something else they could use to show the tourism board that Dry Creek was an exciting town worthy of visitors.

"Who wants to look at an old stop sign anyway?" Charley finally said.

Mrs. Hargrove nodded. "It's too bad I'm not still planting the field of pansies every spring. There's a place in southern California that charges people to look at its field of flowers—ranunculus, I think—we could have the same sort of thing here for free. Maybe I should just plant the field like I used to. That would give something for tourists to see."

"You mean the field in back of your farm?" Charley asked with a frown. Mrs. Hargrove lived year-round in her house in Dry Creek these days and no longer spent the summers on the farm she'd worked with her late husband. "You leased that land to

Curt, remember? I think he wants to plow it up this spring and plant it with wheat. I don't think he'd like people tramping through his wheat."

"It's the hillside on the edge of the field that I'd use. It's too steep for wheat. You'd never get a combine in to harvest a crop. Besides, I was only saying if. *If* doesn't mean when."

The two of them stopped to drink a little more coffee and think. Mrs. Hargrove finally noticed how dim it was and stood up to pull the chain on the light over the table.

Charley grunted in appreciation of the light. "Those pansies of yours were always something."

Mrs. Hargrove used to love to plant her field of pansies in the early spring. It had been a tradition in Dry Creek for the past forty years for the mayor to give out pansies to the local mothers on Mother's Day. When the town started giving out the pansies, Mrs. Hargrove grew all of the flowers. Now her arthritis bothered her and she had given up raising the flowers ten years ago when she had stopped moving to the farm for the summers. No one else in Dry Creek had volunteered to do the planting, so the town bought tiny blooming pansies in paper cups from some store near Billings.

It was a poor substitute in Mrs. Hargrove's opinion. "A flower should be grown with love—and big enough to see. Those paper cup ones are puny. A wind would blow them over."

"Still, we can't stop giving out the pansies," Charley said. "It's thankless enough to be a mother, we can't take away their pansies. I remember when my wife used to get one of your pansies. She would talk about where to plant that thing for days before she actually got it. She had me digging holes all over the place."

"Not many towns give out pansies to every single mother who lives there. Now, that's tradition for you," Mrs. Hargrove said with satisfaction. "It could also be an attraction for visitors if we had a flower field. Folks love to look at flowers."

Charley grunted. "There might even be a

picture in something like that. The guide-book people said they'd like a picture for the students to use."

"Maybe if we focus on the pansies, that tourist board will forget about our stop sign," Mrs. Hargrove said. "After all, the sign is all rusted out. It would make a ter-rible picture. It's a wonder the thing hasn't fallen down by now."

Charley nodded. "It would be a blessing if it did. I think it would fall down if folks stopped piling rocks around the bottom of it."

Neither one of them said much more. Mrs. Hargrove offered Charley some oatmeal-raisin cookies to go with his coffee and he only ate two, explaining his appetite just wasn't with him. Mrs. Hargrove said she understood.

The information for the guidebook wasn't due until June, so Mrs. Hargrove and Charley decided to let the matter rest for a while.

Over the next couple of months, Mrs. Hargrove's mind kept going back to the fateful day when the Nelsons and the Hargroves had forbade their children to marry.

Mrs. Hargrove knew she and her late husband had had good intentions just like the Nelsons had. Mrs. Hargrove had thought she was doing the best thing by sending Doris June off to Anchorage to live with her aunt and refusing to give Curt the address when he asked for it.

Mrs. Hargrove had no idea Doris June would never marry and that Curt would get so angry at his folks for interfering that he'd sign up with the army just to leave home and later make a disaster of the one marriage he entered into.

As the winter wore on, Mrs. Hargrove and Charley felt so miserable about the mess they'd made of things all those years ago that they could barely face each other. Mrs. Hargrove lost her appetite and stopped cooking for herself. Every once in a while, she would open a can of soup without even checking the label, but that seemed to be all she could do. Charley missed the cookies Mrs. Hargrove used to make for him. Finally, they both knew something had to be done to set things right again before they wasted away.

"If we could unmatch them back then, we should be able to match them up again now," Charley finally said one morning.

"It won't be that easy." Mrs. Hargrove didn't need to ask who Charley was talking about and she felt relieved that he had finally suggested they do something. She'd been thinking nonstop about the situation, but she hadn't gotten any ideas about anything solid that she could do.

"It might be easier than we think to get them together. It's not like either one of them is seeing someone else," Charley said. "And they're not shy."

Mrs. Hargrove stopped moving and thought a minute. "It's not a matter of shyness. We'd have to get them in the same place at the same time. That'd be the challenge. I've never seen two people more determined to avoid each other. Doris June won't even visit me unless it's the middle of summer or harvest season when she knows Curt is too busy to come into town."

"I don't think they've even talked to each other in all these years," Charley said.

"Well, certainly not while Curt was married to that woman. Doris June was furious."

"Did she say that?"

"She didn't have to. I know my daughter."

"Well, she doesn't need to worry about the woman Curt married. She ran off with some man the day after she put Ben in kindergarten. The only time Curt heard from her after that was when he got the divorce papers. You'd think she'd at least contact her own son over the years, but she hasn't and here Ben just turned fifteen last month. A boy like that needs a mother."

Mrs. Hargrove wouldn't say it, but she knew Ben needed a grandmother, too. "He's a good boy. I'm sure Doris June would like to get to know him better. I don't know what would make her agree to be in the same room with Curt, though."

Charley thought a minute. "One of us could pretend we were dying. They'd both come to see us then."

Mrs. Hargrove stood still and thought a moment. She almost wished she could do it, but she knew better. "Nothing good ever comes of telling a lie."

"Well, maybe we don't need to be dying," Charley conceded as he rubbed his chin in thought. "But we could still need some help—after all, we're both in our seventies. That should be reason enough to give us some help if we needed it."

"I'll not be asking Doris June for money. She already tries to give me more than she should."

"No, money won't work. Besides, it's too easy to write a check. She wouldn't even need to come home to do that."

"But what else do we need help with except money?"

Charley thought a moment. "Lifting. What we need to do is find something that needs lifting."

"Doris June will just tell me to save the lifting until she comes in the fall."

"Well, maybe it's something that needs to be lifted before fall gets here."

"The pansies," Mrs. Hargrove said with

a smile. "If I get some seeds in the ground soon, we'd have them by May."

"A pansy's not very heavy," Charley said skeptically.

"They will be if we do pansy baskets this year," Mrs. Hargrove said. Her eyes started to shine with excitement. "I saw some gardening show on television a few months ago and it showed these big beautiful pansy baskets. I thought at the time how impressed everyone would be if we could hand out baskets like that for Mother's Day. And it's not just the baskets. If we grow the pansies from seed there will be lots of heavy work. There'll be bending and lifting—and digging. Besides, the pansies could be a tourist attraction, too."

"Maybe so. That hillside used to be something to see when you grew the pansies in the past," Charley said. "My wife used to call it a carpet of lavender. Pure poetry it was."

"There's nothing like the color of a pansy," Mrs. Hargrove agreed. She was pleased Charley had noticed her flowers. Not all men did. "To fill up those big baskets, I'll need to plant even more pansies than I used to plant. And the week before Mother's Day, we'll need to dig up hundreds of pansies and put them into baskets. Lots of dirt and shoveling. And me with my arthritis. How can Doris June not come?"

"And Curt would never let you do that kind of work, regardless of whether or not Doris June comes," Charley agreed with a slow smile. "Of course, if she does come, they'll have to see each other. A person can't dig in a flower bed next to someone and not say hello. You know, this just might work—if Doris June comes."

Mrs. Hargrove grinned. "Oh, she'll come."

"Won't Doris ask why Curt doesn't just do all the baskets for you? She knows he's back on the farm."

Mrs. Hargrove shook her head. "Oh, no, she'd have to mention his name to ask and she never does that—not even if I mention it first."

Charley frowned. "You mean she's never asked about him?"

Mrs. Hargrove shook her head. "Not even before he got married."

Charley looked even more troubled. "Maybe that means she's not interested in him. It was a long time ago."

Mrs. Hargrove was silent for a minute. "Well, we don't know if Curt is still interested, either."

"He might not admit it, but he's interested," Charley said. "Ever since he moved to the farm three years ago, I've noticed that the month of June is torn right off the kitchen calendar every year—before the month even starts it's gone."

"Curt was the only one who used to call Doris June just plain June," Mrs. Hargrove said. "Remember, he called her his June bug."

"I'd forgotten about that," Charley said. "He must have been six or seven when he started calling her that. He used to love to tease his June bug."

"I think they might have always loved each other," Mrs. Hargrove said. "And if Curt is still worried about a word on a calendar, there's hope."

Mrs. Hargrove smiled. It was time to plant her pansies. She'd wait until the seeds were sprouted to ask Doris June to come help her. She didn't want her daughter to fret about this trip for any longer than necessary, and fret she would, especially when she realized that the pansies were being grown on land Curt was now leasing.

In the meantime, there were things to do.

It wouldn't hurt for Doris June to do some shopping before she came. Of course, she'd never go shopping for herself if her mother suggested it. No, Mrs. Hargrove decided, the only thing to do was to ask Doris June to go shopping for something for her mother.

Doris June would love that. She had never liked the gingham housedresses that Mrs. Hargrove usually wore. Of course, the housedresses were perfectly fine. They were easy to wash and most of them had a zipper in the front so Mrs. Hargrove didn't need to fumble with buttons when her arthritis was acting up.

Besides, in Mrs. Hargrove's opinion, Doris June had no right to complain about the fashion of others, not when all she ever seemed to wear were business suits. It was a frustration to a mother when she had a daughter as beautiful as Doris June who seemed determined to hide that fact from everyone.

To begin with, Doris June had good bones and good posture. She stood tall and confident. Her hair was a honey-blond and she didn't make the mistake of bleaching it lighter, hoping it would become that Hollywood blond that actresses seemed to favor. Doris June's skin was clear and her blue eyes looked straight ahead at life. She didn't wear much makeup, but she didn't need to.

Doris June was a classically featured woman. Sometimes, though, Mrs. Hargrove worried that her daughter didn't look as young as she should. Before all of that elopement business, Doris June had looked like every other teenage girl. She'd bounced. She'd chattered. She'd even worn some kind of bright blue fingernail polish at the time. But after the elopement—well,

Doris June just didn't seem the same. She stiffened up.

She walked instead of bouncing. She was patient and long-suffering. Mrs. Hargrove couldn't help but notice that her daughter had started to dress like an old lady. Not that she wore housedresses like Mrs. Hargrove did. She would never do that. But Doris June stopped wearing anything that seemed youthful. She still had all the looks she needed to grab the attention of any man she wanted. It's just that, once she had their attention, they were more likely to think of her as a good neighbor or a good employer than a romantic partner.

Mrs. Hargrove decided it was too late to worry about the bouncing. At forty-two, Doris June would have outgrown that by now anyway. But Mrs. Hargrove figured she could do something about the suits Doris June always wore. She had suits in black, gray and navy, and she wore them with white blouses. She always looked crisp, but even Mrs. Hargrove knew clothes like that encouraged a man to think of a tax audit rather than a candlelight dinner.

Mrs. Hargrove felt too guilty to ever talk to Doris June about the kind of clothes she wore, but a mother noticed certain things even if she didn't know what to do about them. Maybe she could do something now, though, if she had Doris June go shopping for her. If she wanted to get Doris June to buy some new clothes for herself, she had to get her into different stores than the ones where she usually shopped, so she wouldn't ask her to buy more gingham dresses. No, she'd ask Doris June to get her a spring dress or two that had some style.

While she was there, Doris June might even pick up some high heels for herself. It wouldn't hurt to remind Curt that Doris June had nice legs.

Yes, Mrs. Hargrove thought, this just might work.

CHAPTER TWO

DORIS JUNE HARGROVE looked up from the contracts she had in front of her. She managed the advertising traffic in the main television station in Anchorage and she often had ad contracts on her desk. Usually, she knew exactly what contracts were in front of her, but ever since the telephone call from her mother two hours ago she hadn't been able to concentrate.

She had suspected for months that something was wrong with her mother. After Christmas, her mother had sounded depressed in their twice-weekly telephone calls and then, in the last couple of months, her mother had sounded too cheerful. Doris June asked her mother if the doctor had given her any new prescriptions and her mother had said no, so Doris June decided her mother must have just had cabin fever and was growing happier as spring started to take hold in Dry Creek.

Doris June hadn't spent a winter in Dry Creek for years, but she remembered the bitter cold well enough to understand how her mother's mood might improve as everything started to thaw. Even Anchorage tended to be milder than southern Montana in some winters.

Of course, the winter wouldn't explain everything. Her mother still wasn't eating right. These days, if Doris June asked her mother what she'd had for lunch, her mother would say she had a can of soup; and she wouldn't even know what kind of soup it was. That wasn't like her mother.

Doris June wished she had a penny for every time her mother had told her that there was too much salt and too little nutrition in canned soup and that it didn't take much time or trouble to make a pot of vegetable soup so there was no excuse for just opening a can.

It was the endless cans of soup that made Doris June start to worry that her mother was sick. But then, in this latest call, her mother had asked Doris June to go shopping before she flew home. She had already bought a ticket for May tenth at her mother's request so she didn't see any problem in picking up a few things for her mother.

Doris June had shopped for her mother before and knew just where to find the housedresses that her mother liked. She even knew the colors her mother liked; they never varied. Nothing about her mother's wardrobe varied. But this time her mother didn't want a gingham housedress; she wanted a frilly, spring dress.

"In cotton?" Doris June had asked, bewildered.

"No, cotton's too plain."

Cotton's too plain. Doris June had wondered if she'd heard right. Her mother swore by cotton. It's all she ever wanted to wear except for an old wool suit that she brought out for weddings and funerals. She'd never asked for anything else.

"I'm thinking of some of that floaty material you see people wearing in magazines these days," her mother continued.

"You mean like chiffon?"

"Yeah, something like that," her mother said. "Something that swishes and swirls when you turn. In some pretty colors. Maybe rose or violet."

"You mean like the stuff they use when they make prom dresses?"

"Yeah, that would work."

"It doesn't sound very durable," Doris June said. *And what had happened to navy gingham housedresses with zippers?*

"Well, we don't always need to be practical. A woman needs a pretty dress or two. And buy something for yourself while you're at it—something that isn't a suit. Something that floats."

"You're sure you don't want me to come home before the tenth?" Doris June asked after a moment. Her mother had already asked her to come and help with the traditional Mother's Day pansies. Doris June didn't understand why her mother needed help with a few plants, but if her mother asked for help, Doris June would drop everything to go. She had a plane reservation to leave next Tuesday, but she could change her plans.

"Oh, don't come early." Her mother sounded alarmed. "We won't be ready for you."

"We?"

"Well, Charley's going to help me start the baskets. I won't need your help until the tenth."

Doris June was dumbfounded when she hung up the phone after the conversation ended. When she combined the mood swings with the erratic behavior and the talk of dresses in chiffon material, she finally realized what it all must mean.

Her mother wasn't sick: she was going senile.

That must be why her mother had stopped cooking for herself and had become obsessed with planting pansies.

Come to think of it, her mother had said months ago she and Charley were going to put off the work they had to do for the tourism board. Doris June hadn't heard a mention of it since. Her mother wasn't the kind of woman to keep anyone waiting for months for a few pieces of information, especially not an official group like the state tourism board. The woman who raised Doris June would turn that work around in a heartbeat.

Yes, something was wrong.

Even the pansies seemed to be an odd idea now that Doris June thought about it. Her mother hadn't planted pansies for the past ten years. And, with her arthritis, why start again now? Was her mother having some kind of a flashback to a happier, simpler time?

Doris June wondered if her mother had been showing other signs of confusion. Her mother hadn't been putting together any puzzles lately, either. She used to do dozens of puzzles every winter. Maybe the thousand-piece puzzles were suddenly too hard for her.

Doris June made a mental note to pick up some hundred-piece puzzles while she was out shopping. A few puzzles that weren't too challenging for her mother were certainly better things to buy her than some chiffon dress. Where would her mother even wear a dress like that?

Doris June decided she would also stop

by her doctor's office and see if they had any information on the signs of early dementia. Maybe there were some mental exercises her mother could do or some special vitamins she could take.

Doris June knew her mother didn't have severe problems. If she were exhibiting really bizarre behavior, it would be obvious to everyone and someone from Dry Creek would call Doris June and tell her about it.

Doris June took a deep breath and made herself relax. It wasn't anything earthshaking. Older people often found themselves a little confused. Her mother was probably at the place where she needed to start making adjustments in her life. It was nothing to cause any major alarm. It was simply a part of the aging process. Her mother believed in being practical about such things, and Doris June had no doubt her mother would take her diminished sharpness in stride.

Doris June was just glad she would be able to give her mother some more help during the whole process. It might even bring her and her mother closer together, Doris June decided. Her mother had been the strong one her whole life; it was natural that the positions would reverse themselves and Doris June would become the one who was strong for her mother, instead.

THE NEXT WEEK, on the Nelson farm just outside of Dry Creek, Charley pulled a chair up to the old table that stood squarely in the middle of the kitchen. Over the years, the stove in the kitchen had been replaced twice and the refrigerator three times. The cupboards had been refaced and the floor retiled. The one thing that hadn't changed, though, was the table. He had sat down to breakfast at the same table in the same chair for the past forty years.

For some of those years, Charley had wondered if his life was in a rut. A man ought to see some change over the years, he figured, or there was no point in being alive.

When his son, Curt, moved home to take over the farm duties, Charley thought about relocating to someplace else, like maybe Florida or even just into the town of Dry Creek itself. He got maps and a book on the best places to retire. Then he realized he had everything he wanted in this small piece of Montana farmland and there was no reason to move anywhere else.

He'd had no reason since then to regret his decision to stay.

Watching the haggard look leave Curt's face and seeing Ben fill out like a normal healthy teenager was something Charley wouldn't miss for all the beaches in Florida. The big city of Chicago had taken its toll on his son and grandson, and Charley was glad they had returned to their roots.

Breakfast was Charley's favorite meal because all three Nelson men sat down together just like they were going to do this morning. It was seven o'clock and Ben was just coming in the kitchen door after feeding the horses. Curt was standing in front of the stove getting ready to flip the eggs.

Charley hated to catch Curt in a moment when he needed his concentration, but sometimes a man had to think about the greater good even if it meant a yolk got broken.

"I just wish Ben could have been alive

to see you making your traditional Mother's Day breakfast for his grandmother," Charley said. "You did it every year. A boy should know what his family's made of."

"No big secret there. We're probably made of fried eggs and pancakes by now," Curt said as he turned one of six eggs on the same griddle he'd used a little earlier to make pancakes. Fried eggs and pancakes were about as advanced as the cooking got at the farm, although Curt could make a good bowl of chili as well.

"If I remember right you made some fancy French toast one Mother's Day. What was it you put in it?"

Curt grinned. "I put cinnamon on top of it. I thought I was really the gourmet chef."

Charley smiled. "And you had some real maple syrup. Your mother talked about that syrup for days. She couldn't figure out where you'd gotten a bottle of the stuff."

"Billings," Curt said as he turned another egg with a flourish. "I bribed Mr. Dennison and he brought it out for me when he did the mail route."

"How come we never have French

toast?" Ben grumbled as he pulled his own chair out. He'd just washed his hands and he wiped some of the dampness on his jeans before he sat down on the chair and pulled it close to the table.

"I only made it that one time for Mom," Curt said as he reached up into the cupboard and grabbed a platter.

"I wish I'd been there," Ben said quietly.

Charley had never seen a more wistful boy than Ben. Charley had thought Ben would outgrow it when he was on the farm, but he hadn't yet. The boy always looked like he was missing something. And he was too quiet. He didn't yell and shout like most teenagers, not even at basketball games.

"I wish you'd been there too, son," Curt said as he put the turner under a couple of eggs and slid them onto the platter. The pancakes were keeping warm in the oven. "I wish it more so you could have met your grandmother than because my French toast was anything special."

"Your grandmother was real tickled when you were born," Charley added. One of the sad facts of his life was that his wife had died a few months after Ben was born and, due to her sickness, had never seen Ben. If the boy's grandmother had lived, she would have known what to do to make Ben feel he had whatever it was he was missing.

"I always like to think Grandma would have been something like Mrs. Hargrove," Ben said.

Curt set the platter of eggs and pancakes in the middle of the table and pulled out his own chair. "Your grandmother was not quite as opinionated as Mrs. Hargrove."

"There's nothing wrong with a woman having opinions," Charley said. He knew Curt still had hard feelings for all of the Hargroves, but he kept hoping someday Curt would soften his views on Mrs. Hargrove. Charley counted the woman as one of his best friends and it rankled that his son didn't respect her as he should.

Curt grunted. "She can have opinions as long as she keeps them to things she knows about."

"I can't imagine that there's much that Mrs. Hargrove doesn't know about," Charley said. She had tended his broken leg and made him a salve that killed the pain better than the pills the doctor had given him. That had to count for something.

Curt snorted. "I can think of a thing or two she doesn't know." Curt stopped and looked over at his son. Curt swallowed and his voice was milder when he spoke again. "Of course, we all respect her for what she does for the community."

Charley nodded. He was glad Curt could rein in his annoyance. "Mrs. Hargrove has a way with children."

"She's always nice to me," Ben said. "I like her."

Ben was looking at his father with a big question in his eyes and Charley could see that Curt was holding his tongue. Charley was glad that he and Mrs. Hargrove had decided to do something to try and fix the hard feelings they had caused all those years ago. If Curt's feelings about Mrs. Hargrove were anything to go by, there were still some unresolved issues.

"The Hargroves were always our best and closest neighbors," Charley finally said.

Curt clenched his jaw briefly before relaxing it. "And Mrs. Hargrove always charges me a fair price for leasing her land."

Charley nodded. "She'd rather rent that land to you than anyone."

"It's good land."

Charley thought he'd begun his conversation satisfactorily. He didn't want to force Curt in any direction; he just wanted to give him time to think. "We have a lot to be grateful for—including these eggs."

Curt looked at his father and took the cue. "Well, let's eat then so Ben isn't late catching the school bus."

Curt decided he would eat his pancakes and forget about the Hargroves. There was a minute's worth of silence when he thought his strategy was working.

"I bet Mrs. Hargrove can make French toast," Ben said as he slipped a second pancake onto his plate. "She's probably got a recipe and everything."

"I'm sure she does," Curt said as he took the platter that Ben passed his way and looked up at the clock. "You're going to have to get ready for the bus soon."

"I've got time," Ben muttered. "I'd even have time to eat French toast for breakfast if we ever had it."

"Well, Mrs. Hargrove has offered to cook us dinner when we help her with those Mother's Day baskets," Charley said from the other side of the table. "If we wanted to make it French toast, I'm sure that would be fine."

"We don't want to waste one of Mrs. Hargrove's dinners on something I can make myself with a few pointers," Curt said as he cut into the pancake on his plate. "I still remember the lasagna she used to make."

Curt wasn't sure exactly when he had agreed to help Mrs. Hargrove plant her pansies, but he wasn't sorry that he was doing it as long as he could do it without having to spend too much time in her presence. He had plowed the plot for her six weeks ago and covered the whole thing with a heavy plastic that kept the warmth inside.

Mrs. Hargrove had some solar lights out there and the whole thing made a low-lying greenhouse. He'd been skeptical that it would work until he remembered that Mrs. Hargrove had found a way to grow her pansies years ago in the old days when she didn't even have the solar lights.

"She'd have to drive into Billings to find the ingredients for her lasagna," Charley said. "And you know her car's been having some trouble so she's not driving it that far these days."

"Well, I could drive her into Billings."

Charley looked down at his pancake. Things were working out better than he had hoped. "Wouldn't hurt to make the trip count twice. Someone needs to pick Doris June up this evening."

"Doris June's coming?"

Charley nodded.

"Here?"

Charley nodded.

Curt told himself he should have seen this coming. He knew Doris June didn't usually come home for Mother's Day, but this was a special Mother's Day for Mrs. Hargrove if those pansies were anything to go by. He supposed Doris June would want to spend the day with her mother. He couldn't begrudge her that.

"I'll be happy to lend my pickup to Mrs. Hargrove," Curt said. "No point in two people making the trip to Billings."

Charley nodded. "I'm sure the two of you can work something out."

Curt looked over at his father. The man was innocently eating a second pancake and looking as if he hadn't been anywhere around when the noose had been thrown around Curt's neck.

"Linda from the café might be able to drive Mrs. Hargrove to Billings—she can use my pickup," Curt added. He'd be willing to pay Linda a prime wage to do just that. Doris June liked Linda. She'd be happy to have a ride back to Dry Creek with the young woman. Curt knew Doris June wouldn't like to see him meeting her at the airport. In fact, she might stay on the plane rather than get in a pickup that he was driving.

When Curt moved back to Dry Creek four years ago, he had assumed he would see Doris June again. He had even hoped they might have a nice, quiet conversation about what had happened all those years ago. He knew a hole had been burned through his world the day their elopement fell apart, and he couldn't believe it hadn't affected Doris June as well. There was no ignoring that hole, but maybe if they talked about what had happened, they could become friends again.

At the very least, Curt would like to apologize. He'd been impatient back then when he had pressed Doris June to elope with him. He'd been wrong to pressure her and then wrong to run off and join the army when everything fell apart. He'd started to write her a letter many times, but he never found words that said how very sorry he was if he had hurt her.

He knew he'd hurt himself with his hot-tempered actions. He'd lost the best friend he'd ever had in his life.

Curt knew better than to hope that some-day they could be more than friends. He couldn't believe Doris June would forgive him to that extent. He knew Doris June. She was a very organized woman, and if she had moved him to the "undesirable" section in her mind, she wouldn't likely budge from it later. She had been furious with him when they parted twenty-five years ago, and her silence since then told him all he needed to know about how she felt.

Of course, it hadn't all been his fault. Curt often wondered if Mrs. Hargrove ever told her daughter how many times he had asked for Doris June's address in Alaska and been refused. When he thought about it much later, he couldn't believe that Doris June had forbidden her mother to give him the address, so he laid the blame squarely at Mrs. Hargrove's feet.

And the older woman was still at it. The fact that Doris June went out of her way to avoid seeing him when she came to Dry Creek was not lost on Curt. When she came to visit her mother, Doris June always seemed to know where he was—at least, he assumed she must know where he was because she was never at the same place as he was and, in a town the size of Dry Creek, that could only be intentional. Even if Doris June had not asked her mother back then to refuse to give him her address, she was certainly asking her mother to help her avoid him these days.

It was too bad, Curt told himself as he pushed his chair back from the table and stood up to go get the rest of the pancakes that were in the warm oven. It was definitely too bad. There had been many times over the past twenty-five years when he could have used a friend like Doris June. He liked to believe that she missed his friendship as well. Even if she could never love him again, he wished she could forgive him enough to sit down with him and ask him how his life was going.

Of course, for her to do that she would have to talk to him again and that didn't seem likely. Once Doris June made up her mind about something, it stayed made up. She was one stubborn woman. Just like her mother.

CHAPTER THREE

DORIS JUNE WAITED for the airplane to come to a complete stop at the Billings airport before she unfastened her seat belt. It was dark outside except for the lights on the runway. Other passengers had started to reach for their overhead luggage, but Doris June was content to live by the rules and stay seated. She had a bag of puzzles in the overhead compartment and she'd wait for the line of people to pass before she pulled it down. She'd gotten to the airport at six o'clock this morning anyway and she was tired.

She could also use the few extra minutes to go over in her mind what she intended to say to her mother about the quite understandable possibility that her mother's mental agility was compromised and that her mother might want to be open to receiving some help. Help that Doris June fully intended to give even if she had to pretend to take a series of short vacations to Dry Creek, Montana, to give it.

In her checked luggage, Doris June had a whole packet of information about how to deal with what she had decided to call "senior confusion." She hoped that "confusion" was a friendly, befuddled term that would not hurt her mother's dignity. The one thing that stood out every time she read one of those brochures was that Doris June, being the primary caregiver in the event of anything, should realize her mother needed help and that it should be given as naturally as it would be if her mother had a physical limitation that meant she couldn't walk or see or hear anymore.

There was no cause for shame because a person faced a change in mental ability and Doris June intended to see that that message got through to her mother. Her mother was a proud woman and deserved to keep her pride.

Doris June knew that she was limited in how much help she could give her mother from a distance and she was perfectly willing to spend more time with her mother if that was what was needed. Doris June's job was going smoothly, and she could afford to take a week off every three months or so. She had already mentioned the idea to her boss, and she had his full support. He knew Doris June was all her mother had and he understood the importance of family obligations.

There was nothing to prevent Doris June from flying back to Dry Creek regularly to help her mother with odds and ends—things like filling out the form for the state tourism board or maybe doing her taxes. Even if all she did was make pots of soup for her mother to freeze, Doris June would be happy to do it.

She was even prepared to make the big move and leave her job in Anchorage so she could relocate to Dry Creek. She had thought about doing that anyway before *he* moved back—not that she was exactly staying away because Curt Nelson was back, but she sure didn't want it to look like she was moving back home because he was there all single and available.

If Doris June did move back to Dry Creek, she would want it clearly understood that she was moving back there to do her duty to her mother and for no other reason. The people of Dry Creek had a tendency to gossip about their own and Doris June didn't want to have any speculation that she was coming back to ignite a love that had died decades ago.

She'd had enough pity stares over the years to last her a lifetime. She didn't know why the people of Dry Creek had been so interested in the breakup between her and Curt. People broke up all the time even in a small town in southern Montana.

Besides, Curt had married that woman from Chicago. What was her name?

Not that it mattered, Doris June decided. The only thing important about that wedding was that it should have put a complete end to any speculation about her and Curt. She certainly would never have chased a married man. She knew that she'd be so mad at a cheating man that she wouldn't be able to respect him much less love him even if she did snag his interest.

Doris June picked her purse up from under the seat in front of her.

The real problem was that even though the speculation had died down, the pity hadn't gone away. During the year or so after Curt announced his marriage, the people of Dry Creek treated Doris June as if she was a recent widow. The more sympathy people gave her though the more irritated she got. Her life hadn't turned out the way she'd thought it would, but she didn't need a crowd of people around her reminding her of the fact. She could remember it very well on her own.

She felt betrayed. She had lived her life by rules. She had honored the wishes of her parents when it came to leaving Curt. She had trusted that things would fix themselves if she kept her part of the bargain. She had been patient. And then—boom—Curt had married someone else. That's when she knew she shouldn't have listened to her parents. They had let her down.

Her heart was broken and it was because she had obeyed someone else's rules.

Of course, she could not live her life with

her face turned away from her parents. She wished she could say she'd had an epiphany of understanding somewhere along the line and that she had forgiven her parents; but it wasn't like that. Life had just inched up on her.

Her father had his first heart attack and Doris June had to stay in close contact with her parents.

Her struggle had been very private though. She didn't want others to know how hard it had been for her. It was humiliating that she had cared so much about a man who had not cared enough about her to wait.

She might not have been able to live without talking to her parents, but she could live without talking to Curt again.

Although, it wasn't easy to keep anything from the people in Dry Creek. Many of them mourned with her over Curt and she knew it. Dry Creek was small enough that the loss of one was the loss of all, whether it was a house that burned down or a crop that was lost due to hail.

All the pity for her lost love became awkward, however.

Doris June wished there was a no-sympathy-needed card she could send to others to say that she was fine now and that, while she appreciated their sentiment, she didn't need special treatment. Unfortunately, there was no such card. There also didn't seem to be any time limit on the sympathy. People still treated her as if she had reason to be upset at any mention of Chicago or brides or weddings.

In fact, Doris June usually didn't get a wedding invitation in the mail like everyone else. Instead, it would be delivered by hand to her mother with instructions to only give it to her if her mother thought she could handle it.

If there was any justice anywhere in the world, the people of Dry Creek would forget all about the day she and Curt had started to elope only to end up in the sheriff's office with a bent fender on the Nelsons' old field pickup and a swirl of angry parents buzzing around them.

Curt hadn't even been going fast when

he hit the signpost. Neither one of them knew there was a signpost there. They found out later that the highway maintenance crew had just come into Dry Creek the day before to put up the sign as a precaution.

Fortunately, the sheriff who had helped them that night had retired years ago, moving to Florida. He had been the only one to witness the tears she had cried when Curt, angry with his parents for what he saw as their interference, had stomped off and left her at the sheriff's office alone to face the remaining questions about the accident. She didn't want to ride back home with her parents and had asked a classmate to come and get her. That classmate had proved a poor choice and within days the story of how Curt had left Doris June sitting at the sheriff's office was all over the school.

Doris June hoped the gossip about that day was dead and buried. Twenty-five years seemed long enough to make it a forgotten subject.

Besides, by now everyone in Dry Creek

probably expected her to move back to help take care of her mother. They knew Doris June took her duties in life seriously and they would assume she would fulfill this one when the time came. Hopefully, she was old enough that people would no longer think she was interested in marriage.

Of course, Doris June didn't exactly know what she would do with all her time if she did move back to Dry Creek. She had her master's degree in business and was accustomed to the pace of a multimillion-dollar sales department; she could hardly spend her days doing nothing more than dicing vegetables and making soup.

Maybe she could start a small business helping people do their taxes or something. There were enough ranchers in the area to bring in a fair amount of that kind of business and Doris June thought she'd enjoy it. She'd grown up on a small ranch and would enjoy helping ranchers with their books. Maybe she could even offer them some suggestions to improve their operations.

The airplane was completely stopped and people were moving down the aisle to the exit by the time Doris June smoothed back her hair and stood up. She had looked in a mirror in Seattle so she knew she looked competent in her white blouse and navy pantsuit.

Doris June had never been able to get away with the breezy flyaway-hair look that was so popular. On other women, the style made them look like they were having spontaneous fun; on her it just made her look a little startled or a little sick or both.

It was a pity really, Doris June thought as she watched a young woman with that style look up to share a smile with the man beside her. Smiles like that never seemed to come to competent-looking women in suits.

Of course, Doris June reminded herself, she had had her wild romantic adventure when she was seventeen and look how it had turned out. It was a disaster. She wondered if that man smiling down at the young woman had any more staying power in him than Curt had had years ago.

The aisle was almost cleared by the time Doris June reached up and got her bag of puzzles from the overhead bin and then started walking toward the exit.

"Excuse me, miss," someone said when she was halfway down the aisle.

Doris June looked down and saw a frail-looking older woman. "Can I help you?"

"I was wondering if your airline will give me my full frequent flyer miles since I started in Seattle."

"I'm sorry, but I'm not a flight attendant," Doris June said as she looked down at her clothes. Maybe navy and white wasn't the best thing to wear today. "There's a flight attendant by the door as we leave though."

Doris June offered a hand to the older woman to help her stand.

"Why, thank you, dear," the woman said as she stood. "You'd make a lovely flight attendant, you know."

Doris June smiled. There was nothing wrong with being seen as someone who helped others. She hoped her mother would be as grateful for a little assistance as this other older woman was.

Doris June knew where the luggage-claim area was and she knew the area outside the terminal doors where she always met her mother. Her mother had promised she would have someone come with her to the airport. Billings was too far away from Dry Creek for Doris June to feel comfortable with her mother making the trip alone, especially at night. With her possible confusion, she might take a wrong turn and get lost.

Not that Doris June would mind waiting for her mother, but she knew her mother would be distressed if she wasn't at the airport when she had said she would be. Her mother liked to be very precise about things like that.

Doris June was surprised when her mother had quickly agreed to have someone come with her to the airport. It showed how fragile her mother had become. Usually, her mother insisted on doing everything herself.

Doris June stacked her two suitcases on

a rolling cart and had them with her when she spotted her mother outside the terminal door. She walked through the wide door and hugged her mother.

Doris June tried to keep the anxiety out of her eyes as she gave her mother a once-over. To her relief, her mother didn't look like she'd lost weight and her eyes were clear of the confused look Doris June had feared she'd see. Maybe all of her worrying had been unnecessary, Doris June hoped.

"We're parked in the lot over there." Her mother pointed vaguely to the right as she seemed to develop a sudden fascination with Doris June's suitcases. "That green's a nice color. Easy to spot on the luggage carousel. They look heavy, but that won't be a problem. Curt said he'd keep an eye out for us and bring the pickup around front when he sees you've come out of the airport."

Doris June froze. Her mother knew that Curt was the last person Doris June ever wanted to see again. Her mother couldn't have forgotten what had happened, could she?

Maybe her mother really was getting

senile, Doris June thought as she looked up.
She hadn't really believed it was possible
until now. But that was the Nelson pickup
all right. She recognized it because it was
what Charley always drove when Doris
June visited Dry Creek. Curt never came
into town on those days. Doris June felt
they had a truce of sorts. She avoided him
and he avoided her. He would never violate
that by expecting her to ride with him from
Billings to Dry Creek. Her mother must be
wrong. "Don't you mean it's Charley who
came with you?"

"Oh, no, dear. Charley doesn't drive
long distances anymore. The road from his
ranch to Dry Creek is as far as he usually
goes."

It was a warm spring night, but Doris
June felt cold.

"Isn't Charley's grandson—what's his
name? Ben—isn't he about the age when
he can drive?"

The pickup was turning into the lane and
making its way toward them.

"Ben's only got his learner's permit."

The pickup was still coming toward them. "Maybe I could find a cab."

"Don't be silly," her mother said as she waved at the pickup. "That would cost a fortune."

Doris June nodded. She needed to think more logically. There was a solution. "I could get a rental car though."

A car passed the pickup and the light from its headlights let Doris June see through the windshield of the pickup. She could tell it was Curt at the wheel. She hadn't seen the man for twenty-five years, but she'd know his face in her sleep. Not that she ever saw him in her dreams, of course. She might have glimpsed him a time or two in her nightmares, but that was all. She was completely over him.

CURT WISHED HE was anyone else. It might be night out, but Doris June was standing under a security light and he saw the dismay on her face before she turned to say something to her mother. She had obviously just heard who had driven her mother to the airport to pick her up. When you've been childhood playmates with someone, you learn to read their body language. And Doris June was holding herself so stiff she looked like she would break.

It was because of this very thing that he'd asked Mrs. Hargrove to take his pickup and go to Billings. Mrs. Hargrove had been a rancher's wife and Curt had been sure the older woman would remember how to drive a pickup with a stick shift, but she had looked so confused when she asked which pedal was the clutch that he hadn't dared encourage her to drive. He'd gone over to the café and offered to pay Linda and tend her place in her absence if she would only drive in with Mrs. Hargrove for him. Linda had shown little remorse as she let him down, even when he offered to sweeten the deal with an extra fifty-dollar bill.

So here he was pulling up to the curb beside Doris June and her suitcases. She had changed since the last time he'd stopped to pick her up twenty-five years ago. Back then, she'd thrown an old flowered duffel bag in the back and given him a knee-bending kiss before climbing into the passenger side of the old Ford pickup his father used to have for hauling small amounts of feed around.

Curt had been granted the use of that pickup when he turned sixteen and he had planned to drive it to Las Vegas with no hesitation. As he recalled, he hadn't even known the thing had no insurance. Not that something like that would have stopped him and Doris June back then. They were in love and impatient to be married. Practical concerns like insurance and finishing high school hadn't entered into their minds.

Curt could still remember the intensity of the feeling though it had been twenty-five years ago. The only time he had come close to that overwhelming feeling of love was the first time he'd held his son in his arms.

Curt couldn't help but wonder if Doris June remembered the feeling like he did. He swore they could have lived on that feeling for the rest of their lives if things hadn't gone so bad so fast.

After he'd hit the stop sign while trying

to steal another kiss from Doris June, everything had changed. The only part of it that he had ever been able to make right was to pay for the repairs to the fender of his dad's pickup. He had sent the money home from the first pay he had received in the army. He knew his father might not use the money to fix the fender, but Curt felt good knowing he had paid for it anyway. He only wished the other problems of that accident had been as easy to resolve.

"Curt was kind enough to drive me in to get you," Mrs. Hargrove chirped as Curt stepped down from the cab of the pickup and walked around the front of his vehicle. He wondered what made the older woman try so hard to be cheerful. The Mrs. Hargrove he knew never put on an act and he couldn't help feeling that her upbeat voice was forced.

"I could have rented a car at the airport," Doris June said stiffly. "I wouldn't have wanted you to bother."

"It was no bother." Torture maybe, Curt thought, but bother? No.

If it was just him and Doris June in the

pickup, Curt would have used the darkness of this ride to tell her that he was a hundred kinds of sorry. But, as sorry as he was, he wasn't about to bare his soul in front of Mrs. Hargrove. A man had to have some dignity.

MRS. HARGROVE HAD about run out of things to say and the pickup hadn't even passed the sign that signaled the exit from the airport. It was a bonus that the pickup only had the one seat and Doris June was forced to sit between her and Curt, but Mrs. Hargrove did admit that it made the conversation somewhat strained as Doris June insisted on looking straight ahead. On her lap, Doris June kept the large shopping bag that she'd carried off the plane, so it was almost impossible for Mrs. Hargrove to look over and see Curt's face.

Charley would have been much better at this part of it, Mrs. Hargrove fretted as she remarked for the second time that the night was unusually dark and that it looked like the moon was covered with clouds so maybe it would rain tomorrow. Unfortu-

nately, Charley was back at his ranch playing a board game with his grandson and so
the conversation fell to Mrs. Hargrove.

Mrs. Hargrove was never one to shirk
her duty, no matter how unpleasant, but it
was very difficult to keep a conversation
going all by herself. If it wasn't so important to set the tone for Doris June's visit
home, she would have been content to let
her daughter and Curt sit there without a
friendly word between them.

"Curt has been helping me with the pansies," Mrs. Hargrove finally said. "I don't
know what I would have done without
him."

"It's no problem," Curt mumbled.

"I wish you would have let me come earlier," Doris June said with a quick smile to
her mother. "I'm happy to help you with
whatever you need."

Mrs. Hargrove nodded and patted her
daughter's arm. "And I appreciate it. You're
good to me."

"I'm sure we'll be able to handle the pansies," Doris June said. "Curt probably has

other work he needs to do this time of the year."

"I'm not that busy," Curt said.

"Yes, but—" Doris June began.

"The pansies are too heavy," Curt added. "We're going to be digging them up and putting them in my wheelbarrow before taking them into the old house to put in baskets."

"But they're only flowers," Doris June protested. "How heavy can they be?"

Curt grunted. "I'd never hear the end of it from my father if I let the two of you dig up those pansies and pack the baskets by yourselves."

"Well, we will pay you then," Doris June said crisply. "Let us know your rate."

"I don't have a rate. The baskets are for the town. And for Mother's Day! You don't think I'd take money for doing something like that, do you?"

"Of course not," Mrs. Hargrove said hastily. She had tried to let the two of them handle the conversation, but they seemed determined to bury it. "And we appreciate it. Don't we, Doris June?"

Doris June murmured something that could be an agreement.

Mrs. Hargrove couldn't think of anything else to say.

Everyone was silent. The only sound was the pickup engine as it kept humming along.

Doris June tried very hard not to move. She had worn the navy slacks that went with her suit, but the material didn't seem heavy enough when her leg was pressed against Curt's leg. It had been years since Doris June had ridden in the middle place in a pickup and she had forgotten how the gears forced the person in that position to lean their leg against the driver's leg. She could almost feel the texture of the denim of Curt's jeans.

Doris June used to love to ride this close to Curt. Back then, she'd snuggled even closer to him although there was no one sitting on the other side of her like her mother was tonight. For the first time that evening, Doris June found something for which to be grateful. She was glad her mother hadn't just sent Curt in alone to get her from the airport. She wouldn't have had a clue what to say to him if they had been alone.

Doris June hoped the darkness inside the pickup cab hid the flush to her face. She was a highly paid professional; she shouldn't be caught in situations like this, stuck where she didn't want to be. She had a feeling it was going to be a long time until the baskets were ready for Mother's Day.

CHAPTER FOUR

IT WAS DARK when they drove down the road into Dry Creek later that night. Doris June was relieved to be home. The trip from the Billings airport had been so long even her mother had given up on talking.

"When did Linda get a new light for the café?" Doris June asked, relieved to finally have something to say. The café and the hardware store stood on opposite sides of the road. No cars were parked in front of either of the buildings, but the grass was flattened where cars had parked earlier in the day so business looked reasonably good.

"Just after Christmas," Curt answered.

Ah, it was good to see Dry Creek again, Doris June thought to herself as she tried to forget the awkwardness with Curt. She wasn't going to let seeing him spoil her time here. Even the air smelled better in Dry Creek. Maybe it was the scent of spring grasses or the fact that there was so little car exhaust, but it definitely smelled good. She was glad Curt kept his window rolled down a little.

"Well, here we are," Curt said as he pulled into her mother's driveway.

"Thank you so much," Doris June said to Curt, and congratulated herself on handling the whole drive back with gracious good manners. One did not need to chatter away to be polite.

Doris June even managed a brief smile for Curt when he lifted her suitcases out of the back of his pickup and carried them to her mother's porch. She didn't want to encourage him to come inside, so she said another thank-you at the bottom of the stairs leading up to the porch.

Fortunately, it was dark and the nightlight on the porch was dim, so Curt wasn't able to see that she looked at his chin when she gave him her thanks for carrying her suitcases. She knew it wasn't the best of manners, but it was good enough, especially considering Curt only grunted in response to her thanks, so she might as well not have even bothered saying it anyway. He didn't give any hint, either, that he'd like to come inside, which, when Doris June thought about it, made her decide he was halfway rude. The man should at least hesitate before stomping off to his pickup, just in case someone wanted to invite him inside for a cup of coffee or something. Not that anyone did, of course.

With all the thanking, however, Doris June didn't remember her worries about her mother growing senile until she'd hauled her shopping bag full of puzzles into her mother's house and then gone back outside for her suitcases. She didn't even know what clues she should look for to determine her mother's state of mind.

"You've changed the cloth on top of the piano," Doris June said, when she stood beside her suitcases and looked around the living room. She doubted if that was enough to signal a problem. Maybe the fact that her mother hadn't changed the carpet in the past forty years should worry her more than the one single thing she had changed.

"Change is a good thing," Mrs. Hargrove said as she gave her daughter a meaningful look. "We don't have enough of it around here."

That was a good sign, Doris June thought. If her mother's mental ability deteriorated, it would be easier to help her if she was open to change. Doris June hoped her mother really meant what she'd said. "I have been thinking the carpet could be changed."

"The carpet?" Her mother seemed surprised. "What's wrong with the carpet? It matches the sofa."

"Well, maybe a change would be good. Like you said. We could get a new sofa, too."

"But your father picked out that sofa." Mrs. Hargrove looked bewildered. "He said it would wear well with children."

"There hasn't been a child living in this house for over thirty years," Doris June said, and then looked at her mother's face and wished she'd never mentioned the carpet or the sofa.

Her mother appeared to be on the verge of tears. "I'm sorry. It's all my—my fault."

"It's okay. Whatever it is, it's okay." Doris June didn't know what she would do if her mother cried. Her mother never cried. That was a change Doris June had not been prepared to see. "Forget I mentioned the carpet. We don't need to change anything. Everything's okay. And the sofa, it's perfect."

A single tear rolled down Mrs. Hargrove's cheek. "I'm sorry you don't have any children."

"That's okay. Don't worry about a thing." Doris June patted at her suit. Why didn't she have a pocket in these suits so she could carry a tissue around for times like this? "Don't cry. Everything's fine."

Doris June didn't know what the sudden concern about her lack of children was all about, but it had to be a symptom of this senior confusion. Her mother was a strong woman. She never cried about things, especially not things like this that she couldn't do anything about. Doris June told herself she should have come home sooner. Her mother needed her.

"But you don't even date," her mother said as she pulled her own tissue out of the pocket of her housedress.

"I do so date," Doris June said, relieved that one of them had a pocket. "Remember that guy—Bob—I told you about him. I dated him."

"That was years ago."

"Oh." Doris June tried to remember. Had it been that long? "Well, maybe I don't date every man I meet, but I do fine. I'm fine with dating. I could go out tomorrow if I wanted. Well, maybe not tomorrow since I'm here, but if I was back in Anchorage, it could be anytime. I'm fine with dating."

Doris June breathed much easier now that there were no new tears in her mother's eyes. And she was telling the truth. She could date that new weatherman if she wanted. All she would need to do would be to pay the bill for both of them. Which would be fair enough since she was older than him. It would still count as a date, though, wouldn't it? Men paid on dates all the time; a woman could pay, too.

Mrs. Hargrove put her tissue back in her pocket. "So you won't mind if I invite the Nelsons to dinner tomorrow?"

"What?" Doris June looked at her mother. Where had that come from?

"Of course, it would be easier than going on a date for you," her mother said calmly. "Just the Nelson family. You've known them for years."

"You mean Charley? And his grandson?"

Her mother nodded. "And Curt, of course."

"But Curt? Won't he be busy?"

"Charley might have an opinion about the carpet," Mrs. Hargrove offered just as though nothing had been said about Curt.

Doris June nodded. She supposed everyone would have an opinion. If not about the carpet, then about her dating life—or lack thereof.

"And it'll give us a chance to wear our new dresses," Mrs. Hargrove added cheerfully. "You said you got me a couple—and one for yourself, too."

Doris June nodded. She didn't know why she had bought a dress for herself when she picked up the two for her mother. Maybe she thought it wasn't fair to let her mother make a fool of herself alone.

"Well, I can't wait to see us all dressed up."

Doris June didn't say it, but she was quite happy to wait. She could have waited for this dinner for the rest of her life. It wasn't that she was a coward exactly. Well, not totally a coward. There were some very good reasons not to have the Nelsons to dinner and none of them had to do with her dating anyone.

"Curt won't come," she said with relief. "He'll be working late plowing. It's his busy time of the year. Spring."

"Maybe I should make lasagna," her mother said. "It's his favorite."

Of course, Doris June thought to herself. Her mother would have to lure Curt here. Still, there were ways. "I haven't had liver and onions for a long time. Isn't that Charley's favorite? I could drive you to Billings tomorrow if you wanted to get some."

"My car hasn't been working so good."

Doris June didn't wonder at that. Her mother had driven the same car since the seventies; it was bound to die at some point.

"I'll talk to Linda," Doris June said. "She might have some frozen liver at the café. Or maybe she's going in for supplies and could get some fresh for us."

"You really think I should make liver and onions instead of lasagna?"

Doris June nodded. "Curt can buy that frozen lasagna anytime he wants from the grocery store. I bet they eat that once or twice a week. But liver and onions. Where can Charley get that like only you can make it? Besides, it's good to let Charley know you're thinking of him."

In the brochures Doris June had read, it said seniors needed to know they were still important. Charley could probably use some attention, too.

"Well, of course, I'm thinking of him," her mother said with a befuddled look on her face. "He's Charley."

Doris June smiled. Things would work

out just fine. "Oh, and maybe you should tell Charley what the menu is when you invite him. Give him something to look forward to for the day."

"He always asks anyway. He doesn't stand on company manners anymore since he comes so often. But, since it's a special dinner, I'll be sure and mention that it's liver and onions."

Doris June relaxed. Curt hated liver and onions. At least he had when they were growing up and, regardless of how much he might have changed since then, she doubted he had changed his opinion on that. He'd never come to dinner.

Doris June would have felt guilty about depriving Curt of his lasagna dinner, but her mother was apparently inviting Charley to meals frequently and, knowing her mother, she was sending leftovers home to Curt and Ben all the time. In fact, Curt would probably get a pan of lasagna within the month. He might not even need to share it with a whole table of other people. He should be happy she'd suggested the menu she had.

CURT KNEW HE had to go to dinner. When
he had been out plowing this morning, he'd
called himself a coward ten times over for
not talking to Doris June on the ride back
from the airport. A man who had wronged
a friend twenty-five years ago couldn't
let his pride stop him from saying he was
sorry. Besides, last night was as close as
he had come to her in all those years and
she hadn't been able to walk away from
him since she was sitting on the seat next
to him.

When he went in for his noon meal and
his father told him they'd been invited to
the Hargroves for dinner that evening, Curt
figured this was his second chance to talk
to Doris June. He wasn't likely to get another chance to say his piece if he didn't
speak to her now.

After all, it was obvious Doris June
wasn't going to start things off by saying
anything to him. She avoided him like
he had the plague. Actually, now that he
thought about it, she would be friendlier
to him if he did have the plague. She'd be
compassionate to a person with an afflic-

tion like that. But him? He didn't think he could count on her natural kindness when she thought of him.

It was a pity, because if there should be peace between himself and anyone else in the world, that other person was Doris June. He wasn't even thinking of the flare of romantic love they'd shared as teenagers. No, he was remembering back to the solid friendship they'd shared when they were little kids.

It was Doris June who had patiently fished the Big Dry Creek with him and explored the outlines of the old sod buildings where the first Hargroves had lived a hundred years ago. He and Doris June had history together. Doris June had known him better back then than his parents had. When they were nine years old, he had made a pact with her that they would always be blood brothers. She'd been squeamish about using her own blood so he'd generously let her use some of his.

That should have made him realize she wasn't anything like a brother, but he'd simply thought of her as his best friend for several more years. He still remembered the day when they were fifteen and, for the first time, he saw that Doris June was beautiful in a girl way that he'd never appreciated before.

When he thought back, it was amazing that he'd waited until they were seventeen before he'd demanded that they elope. The couples at school were exchanging school rings to wear and he had no patience for that. He knew Doris June so well it seemed strange to ask her to be his steady girlfriend when he already knew he wanted her for his wife.

Back then, everything was black or white. They had not learned to keep secrets from each other or to hold back in saying what they meant. In the years between seventeen and now, though, Curt had developed a healthy respect for the color gray. He wasn't sure he would want to hear all of what Doris June had to say about him now.

Still, a few things needed to be said.

The bad feelings between him and Doris June shouldn't be allowed to continue. Curt looked on this dinner invitation as his chance to fix things. Even though the punch of emotions that had stirred him at seventeen when he thought of Doris June no longer hit him in the same way, Curt knew he needed her forgiveness.

"You got a tie?" Charley had just finished shaving at the sink on the back porch because he said the light was better there. He rubbed some aftershave on his face while he talked to Curt.

"A tie? You think Mrs. Hargrove expects us to wear ties?"

Curt had washed up with farmer's soap at the kitchen sink and the cuffs of his work shirt were wet even though he'd rolled them up to his elbow. Ben was sitting at the table finishing his homework.

"And a white shirt wouldn't be out of place, either," Charley said as he walked back into the kitchen from the back porch. "Something nice."

Curt rolled his sleeves down. "Seems a bit chancy to wear a white shirt when Mrs. Hargrove might serve her lasagna." Out plowing today, when he wasn't worrying over the mistakes of his youth, he'd been thinking about that lasagna.

"Didn't I tell you?" Charley said. "She's making my favorite this time. Fried liver and onions."

"Oh," Curt said as he turned to walk to his bedroom. He might as well wear a white shirt. He sure wasn't going to be spilling any sauce if that's what would be on the table. And a tie wouldn't be much of a problem if he had to wear one of his dress shirts anyway.

There was a slight drizzle as Curt drove the three men into Dry Creek in Charley's car.

"We could stop at the café for pie after dinner," Ben said from the back seat.

"After one of Mrs. Hargrove's dinners?" Charley asked as he turned around to look at his grandson. "She'll have dessert. You can count on it."

Curt looked in the rearview mirror at his son. "Since when did you become such a fan of pie?"

Ben shrugged. "There's cherry."

"I see," Curt said. Something was up with Ben these days, but Curt didn't want to question him. His son was so quiet he didn't want to press him down with questions. Besides, what kind of a question would it be to ask him why he'd all of a sudden grown so interested in pie. Most boys loved pie.

Maybe Ben was just opening his mind to like new things, Curt thought. No one could argue with that.

Before Curt knew it, they were all standing on the porch of the Hargroves house. Charley was getting ready to knock on the door and Curt was running his finger underneath his tie. It felt too tight, but he wasn't complaining. It seemed like men always needed to be uncomfortable when they repented of their sins and Curt was hoping to gain some points with Doris June by looking as miserable as he felt about their problems.

Charley knocked on the door and Mrs. Hargrove answered it.

Curt noticed Mrs. Hargrove was wearing lipstick. Granted, it was a pale pink and it almost looked natural, but it was definitely there. And she wasn't wearing her suit or one of her housedresses. Instead, she had on a turquoise dress with one of those swirly skirts.

"Is there a problem?" Curt asked. She would be wearing black if someone had died, but he couldn't think of any other reason for Mrs. Hargrove to be wearing lipstick. She had to be going somewhere and he knew there were no weddings around.

"No, of course not," Mrs. Hargrove said as she opened the screen door for them. "Doris June is just setting the table."

It took a second for Curt's eyes to adjust to the indoor light. For some reason, Mrs. Hargrove had turned off her overhead light and only had the lamps turned on tonight. It was probably an energy-savings thing, Curt thought. Although, it was just as well the house was a little dim tonight. This was the first time he had been back inside this house in twenty-five years and he didn't want anyone looking at his face too closely.

"Always did like that sofa," Curt said as he looked around. He used to watch television with Doris June on that sofa. He was glad to see that nothing had been changed. Things had kind of faded softly over the years, but they were basically the same. The same flowered wallpaper was on the wall beside the stairs that went up to the second floor. The brick fireplace still had the same brass poker that had turned brown with tarnish.

"They don't build sofas like that anymore," Charley agreed as he walked over and sat down on the thing. Ben followed him.

"Some people think it needs replacing," Mrs. Hargrove said a little louder than was needed.

Curt heard the rattle of silverware coming from the dining room and turned his head toward that room. He was just in time to see Doris June walk out of the dining room. For a second, as she stood in the doorway between the two rooms, framed in the light, her face showed clearly.

Curt hadn't realized that he hadn't really seen Doris June since she'd been home. There'd been no light in the pickup, and even when he dropped her and her mother off last night, the porch light had only shown shapes. If he had thought about it, he would have assumed her face would have softened over the years with the wrinkles and the slight paleness that comes from getting older. He would have been wrong.

She did not glow like the young girl she used to be, but she had a confidence that made her seem even more alive. She was beautiful.

Last night he thought he knew who she was in her conservative pantsuit and sensible shoes. But the vision before him made him forget all his assumptions. He'd pictured Doris June as living a solitary life, but no woman wore a soft, floating pink dress like that one unless she was used to dating and going nice places. He'd been ten kinds of a fool to have spent the day thinking of words to try to mend Doris June's broken heart. She'd obviously mended that heart of her years ago and moved on past him. For all he knew, she didn't even remember that they had packed their bags and headed out for an elopement years ago.

CHAPTER FIVE

DORIS JUNE WAS glad the Nelson men had worn their dress clothes. It made her feel less foolish in the clothes she was wearing. As a rule, people in Dry Creek didn't dress up for any meal except maybe Thanksgiving dinner and here she was dressed up as if she was going to a prom or something and it was only a midweek dinner among neighbors.

Doris June had thought she was making a point by buying the flyaway pink dress with its jagged hem and trailing sleeves. She had hoped to show her mother that there was nothing sensible about such styles. When Doris June suggested her mother expand her wardrobe to include something more than gingham house-dresses, Doris June had meant her mother should also wear some sensible polyester skirts and white cotton blouses. She had not meant that her mother should dress like a teenage party girl.

When Doris June heard her mother ask for this kind of a dress, Doris June didn't believe her mother actually meant it even though her mother had later sent her a picture from a catalogue showing this kind of a dress.

As it turned out, her mother had not only meant for her to buy those kinds of dresses, her mother was also intent on sharing the wealth. Her mother insisted Doris June wear one of the new dresses meant for her instead of the plain gray one Doris June had bought for herself.

The only explanation in Doris June's mind was that her mother was regressing so far back that she was thinking like a thirteen-year-old girl. Unusual behavior like that was definitely up there on the list of symptoms for senior confusion.

Doris June thought she was fortunate she did not have to wear a lamp shade on her head to please her mother. As it was, the pink dress was a little large on Doris June, but it did, at least, look like something a person would wear. Of course, her work shoes had looked foolish next to all the pink froth of the dress, so Doris June had agreed to break in the new slip-ons she had gotten for her mother as well.

If her mother hadn't looked so happy to see her in the pink dress, Doris June would have thought the whole dress thing was just a way for her mother to get someone to wear her new shoes so they wouldn't hurt her own feet when she wore them later.

Doris June looked across the table at her mother. She did look happy.

"More liver?" Doris June picked up the platter closest to her and turned to offer it to Curt.

Doris June decided that the one good thing about wearing shoes that were too tight and a dress that was too short was that it didn't give her a lot of time to worry about how fickle some men could be. Something was wrong with Curt tonight and she didn't know what it was, unless he objected to the dress she was wearing. If she had a minute, she could assure him she thought the dress was ridiculous on someone her age, too. Although now that he was glaring at her as if she'd done something wrong, she probably wouldn't give him the satisfaction of agreeing with him.

"Thank you," Curt said as he slid another piece of meat onto his plate.

Doris June watched him, speechless. He was wearing a tie; he hated ties. He was eating liver and onions; he hated liver and he wasn't overly fond of onions. How could someone have changed so much? The way he'd been looking at her all night, she would have thought he had everything reversed in his mind and thought she should be the one to say she was sorry to him. He seemed to have forgotten who had left whom standing at the sheriff's office.

"Linda had the liver in the freezer over at the café," Mrs. Hargrove said in the same bright voice she had used all evening. "She's thinking about adding liver and onions to the menu if there's enough demand for it."

"I'll have to tell her she has my vote," Charley said. "It's good to change the menu once in a while."

"Her sister, Lucy, says they're selling more kinds of pie, too," Ben added.

Since this was the only bit of conversation Ben had offered for the evening that wasn't required as part of the food-passing process, Doris June thought she should say something to encourage him. Young people could be so shy.

"I bet they serve great pies there," Doris June said with a full-wattage smile for the boy.

Ben looked at her like he appreciated her support and nodded. "Lucy says Linda lets her keep the pie money. Well, on the days when she's working there, at least."

Doris June was pleased to see that Ben was talking.

Apparently Mrs. Hargrove was pleased, too. "I thought I'd seen Lucy working in there."

"Tuesday, Wednesday and Thursday after school and some weekends," Ben said with a nod. "She's saving money to buy a new guitar."

Doris June looked over at Curt to see if

he was noticing how his son was opening up.

"Lucy must be about your age," Mrs. Hargrove said.

Ben nodded. "Almost."

"Didn't you say once that you played guitar, too?" Mrs. Hargrove asked.

Ben nodded.

"Well," Mrs. Hargrove said. "I vote that we go over and get pie after we finish up here. My treat."

"Really?" Ben said.

"Really?" Doris June echoed. She knew her mother had brownies thawing on the kitchen counter.

Mrs. Hargrove nodded. "I always like to encourage young people, and a guitar is a good thing to have. I like to see a young girl who knows what she wants at Lucy's age."

Doris June looked down at the last little piece of liver on her plate. She hoped no one else was thinking what she was—that her mother hadn't been so supportive of her own daughter when she knew what she wanted when she was a couple of years older than Lucy. Of course, there was a difference between a guitar and a husband. Still, the thoughts came and Doris June didn't stop them. She'd missed out on so much. If her mother hadn't interfered, she and Curt would be sitting at this table now and Ben, well, he would be their son.

Not that, Doris June assured herself, she was still pining away for Curt and the life they could have had. Her dream of him had died years ago.

"I can stay and do dishes while you go for pie," Doris June offered. She didn't feel much like walking around Dry Creek with the man who was her dead dream glaring at her the way he had been all evening.

"Nonsense," Mrs. Hargrove said as she set her napkin down on the table. "We could all use the walk over to the café."

Doris June didn't want to argue with her mother even though one hundred steps would do nothing for anyone's exercise routine, especially not if they sat down at the end of the short walk and had a piece of pie.

MRS. HARGROVE DIDN'T understand how Doris June and Curt had ever gotten together as teenagers. Earlier, they had been looking at each other as though they'd never even thought about kissing each other. Mrs. Hargrove and Charley were leading the way over to the café. The day was just sliding into night and so, while there were deep shadows, it was easy enough to find firm footing on the sidewalk leading down to the front gate of Mrs. Hargrove's lawn. From there, they walked on the gravel-sided road toward the café.

"Do you think it's working?" Charley leaned over and asked Mrs. Hargrove softly.

"Ben looks like he's got more romance on his mind than our two kids do," Mrs. Hargrove said in disgust.

Mrs. Hargrove didn't need to turn around to know that Curt and Doris June were walking behind them with a good yard between them and frowns on both of their faces. It was quiet as a tomb so she knew they weren't talking.

"Maybe they need someone to give them the idea," Charley said as he reached over and took Mrs. Hargrove's hand in his.

"Why—?" Mrs. Hargrove stopped walking to look over at Charley in astonishment.

Charley winked.

"Oh, yeah." Mrs. Hargrove swallowed and then smiled weakly. She didn't remove her hand from his, however. Maybe Charley was right, she thought. Maybe their children did need a nudge. She wished she could turn around and see if Curt and Doris June were taking the hint, but she didn't want to be obvious. Children were so sensitive about their parents prying into their romantic lives and Mrs. Hargrove had always been careful not to do that. Well, except for the time she had stopped their elopement, of course.

Mrs. Hargrove sighed at the thought. When she made a mistake, it was always a big one. Not that she could have let them get married. But she could have at least let them write letters to each other. What was the harm in a few letters?

Charley looked over at Mrs. Hargrove and stepped closer so he could put his arm around her.

DORIS JUNE HISSED.

Curt drew back his breath. He was on the verge of saying something to her. Just one word that would start the tumble of his confession. But she hissed. How could he talk when she wasn't paying attention to him? Instead, she was staring straight ahead.

"Did you see that?" Doris June demanded in a low voice as she moved over close enough to him so they could have a private conversation.

Curt hadn't noticed earlier tonight that tiny wisps of hair were escaping Doris June's tightly controlled hair style. But when she stood next to him, he could see the strands of hair lying against her cheek. The strands showed up when Doris June walked under the one streetlight Dry Creek had. It was distracting enough that he hadn't even tried to figure out what she was talking about.

"Huh?" Curt said. He wondered if she'd

be mad if he smoothed those strands back. He'd forgotten how much he used to love the feel of her hair.

"Them." Doris June jerked her head toward something in front of them. "Our parents. Did you see them holding hands?"

"I wasn't watching them. You see I was thinking—" Curt began.

"How could you not see them?" Doris June squeaked. "Your dad had his arm around my mother's shoulder."

Curt decided to try again. "Sometimes when old friends start to feel romantic, things are confusing—"

"You think they're romantic? Our parents?"

Curt could see Doris June was completely missing the point he was trying to make.

"No." Curt figured the only way to get her attention back was to answer her questions. "No, I don't think anyone around here is romantic. But—"

"Of course," Doris June said in a rush. "I should have seen it before now. My mother isn't senile, she's in love. That explains why she wanted me to buy this for her." Doris June held out the skirt of her dress as if there was something wrong with it. "This is probably her idea of a date dress. Why my mother needs a dress like this I don't know. I don't even want to know."

"That dress is your mother's?" Curt smiled in relief. The longer he had looked at that pink frilly dress tonight the more convinced he had been that Doris June must have a regular boyfriend back in Anchorage. A woman wouldn't buy a dress like that unless she had occasion to wear it and wear it often in places that were usually date kind of places.

"You have a problem with the dress?" Doris June asked stiffly.

"Absolutely not, it's a pretty dress," Curt said mildly. He wasn't about to tell her that he'd been worried she had a boyfriend. "But I don't think you have anything to worry about. Things aren't always what you think. Your mom and my dad have known each other for years. They're good friends—that doesn't mean they're romantically inclined."

"So your father has been acting normal lately?"

Curt stopped a moment to think. Now that he knew Doris June didn't own the pink dress, he was enjoying how the breeze blew the sleeves around in the faint light that was coming from that new light Linda had installed on the café porch. He wouldn't mind standing out here and talking for a bit.

"Well, has he been acting normal?" Doris June asked again.

"He might have been a bit preoccupied, I suppose. If one wanted to be technical about it."

Doris June nodded. "My mother, too."

"Maybe they had an argument and were worried about how to fix it between themselves," Curt said, and it could be possible. "I know when friends disagree it can be painful for both people."

"They don't look like they've been fighting."

"Well, but if they had, I'm sure they'd both be sorry and want to say they were sorry. I know I'm sorry about what happened with us."

Curt had to admit his apology lacked any kind of flourish, but it was sincere.

Doris June looked up at him as if he was nuts. "What do we have to do with anything? Look at them."

Doris June pointed ahead of them and Curt decided he had no option except to look. Their parents were standing in the doorway to the café. Light was streaming out around them and they were standing sideways in the door. Their heads were close together and they were talking.

"They're just old friends. That's all," Curt said. He couldn't believe his father and Mrs. Hargrove would change the rules of their friendship after all these years. Besides, he had other things he wanted to talk to Doris June about now that they were alone.

"Your father better not just be stringing my mother along," Doris June whispered up at him fiercely. "That kind of thing runs in your family."

"It does not," Curt protested. "If you're

talking about you and me, you know I wasn't stringing you along. I asked you to marry me."

Doris June snorted, but she did look up at him. "For ten seconds. Then you were off marrying someone else. You never said anything about your proposal expiring. It didn't have the shelf life of a piece of cheese."

"Now, that's not fair. It didn't expire. You wouldn't even talk to me. I didn't know where you were. I couldn't even get an address to write to you."

Curt knew his apology wasn't going well. He probably should have reminded Doris June of the good times they'd had as kids before he talked about their separation, but he was running out of chances.

"Don't worry about it," Doris June said. "It happened a long time ago."

Curt looked down at Doris June's face. The smile she had on looked too much like the kind of smile a person reserved for a difficult customer who came into a store complaining about some milk that had gone bad. It was impersonal and polite. In fact, she wasn't even focusing on him. She was looking at his chin.

"It wasn't that long ago," Curt said. He wished she would look at him. "And I think we still have issues to work out."

Now what had he done wrong? Doris June had stopped even looking at his chin. Instead, she'd turned around and was looking straight ahead at the café. Curt followed the line of her gaze and saw she was still looking at their parents. Curt frowned. His father seemed to be wiping a tear off Mrs. Hargrove's cheek. He didn't know whether he was more astonished that Mrs. Hargrove had shed a tear or that his father was tenderly wiping it away.

"See?" Doris June whispered as she looked up at him.

"I'm sure there's some explanation," Curt said.

"Like what?" Doris June demanded.

Curt squirmed. Now she decided to look him in the eye. "Maybe your mother got a spot of sauce on her cheek from dinner."

"There was no sauce at dinner."

"Well, then, maybe it's the lipstick she was wearing," he said.

"She doesn't wear lipstick on her cheekbone," Doris June answered as she started walking toward the doorway of the café. "And what do you know about lipstick anyway?"

"What is that supposed to mean?" Curt asked, but Doris June was already walking away from him. The doorway to the café was empty. The two older people and Ben had all gone inside. Only he and Doris June were outside and he was wasting his chance to talk with her privately. At the moment, he didn't care if Mrs. Hargrove was crying and his father was turning soft.

"Wait," Curt called as he saw Doris June reach the steps of the café.

She didn't wait, of course, and he had little choice except to follow her inside. He did notice, though, that the light inside the café flashed pink through the material of her dress as she walked through the door. She looked like a sunrise. A sunrise that was moving awfully fast, of course, but a sunrise nonetheless. That was his June bug, all right.

CHAPTER SIX

THE INSIDE OF the café was dimly lit. It had
a floor with black-and-white tiles alternat-
ing across it and big street windows with
white eyelet café curtains covering their
bottom halves. Red-checked cotton cloths
covered all of the tables. Two couples sat
in the front of the café. Linda, the owner,
gestured Mrs. Hargrove and Charley to a
table at the back.

"We'll need room for five," Charley said
as he looked behind him. Ben was inside
the café, but Curt and Doris June were still
halfway outside. Charley hoped that was a
good sign and that they were at least talking to each other by now. This matchmaking stuff was wearing him down and he
wasn't sure how much more of it he could
do, especially because Edith, well, Mrs.
Hargrove, seemed so discouraged by it all.

Charley didn't know why, in the midst of

all their matchmaking plans, he'd started thinking of Mrs. Hargrove as Edith, but he had. Of course, he hadn't said her first name aloud to anyone yet and he wasn't planning to do so. She'd been Mrs. Hargrove to him for too many years to start changing the rules now. Besides, he wasn't sure she'd answer to Edith. Everyone called her Mrs. Hargrove.

Names were a funny thing, Charley thought to himself as he watched Lucy bring an extra chair over to the table where he and Mrs. Hargrove were headed.

"Anyone ever call you by your full name?" he asked the young woman.

"Lucille? Not in years. Why?"

"I just wondered." He also wondered if he should tip Lucy for bringing the chair and decided he would. He wanted to make a contribution to her guitar-buying funds. He wasn't so old that he couldn't appreciate good music.

Besides, even in the dim light of the café, Charley could see that Ben's face was bright pink. Charley figured Ben must have a crush on Lucy and it wouldn't hurt his grandson's cause to give her some money for her effort with the chair. As far as he knew, this was the first girl his grandson had shown any interest in.

"Here." Charley held out the dollar bill he'd pulled out of his suit jacket.

Lucy just looked at the bill. She had her blond hair pulled up in some kind of a fancy ponytail and had tiny red disks dangling from her ears. Ben needed a friend who wore red like that, Charley decided. She would bring him out of his shyness.

"It's a tip for bringing the chair," Charley said as he stepped a little closer to her with the money.

"But you haven't even been served anything yet," Lucy protested. "No one needs to tip when we move a chair around. That's just doing business."

Charley figured it was a good sign that the young woman was so opinionated. The Nelson men always liked strong women who spoke their minds.

"Well, maybe later then," Charley said as he set the dollar bill on the table.

Charley noticed that Ben had already sat

down in the chair that was on the far end
of the table, closest to the kitchen. Charley
looked up to see if Mrs. Hargrove had noticed Lucy and Ben, but he saw by the look
in her eyes that she had her mind somewhere else. He followed her eyes to the
door of the café. Ah, that's what she saw.

MRS. HARGROVE HAD noticed Doris June the
moment she stood, stopped in the doorway.
The color on her daughter's face was high
and Mrs. Hargrove thought that must be
a good thing. She told herself she should
have taken a hand in her daughter's wardrobe long before this. Doris June looked
more kissable in that swirly pink dress than
she had in years and, as her mother, she
should have pointed out the problems with
business suits to her daughter sooner.

"Oh." Mrs. Hargrove noticed in surprise
that Charley was holding out a chair for
her.

"You don't have to—" Mrs. Hargrove
said, and then noticed the flush on Charley's face. She had forgotten they were
setting an example for their children.

She smiled and sat down. "Thank you so much."

Charley sat down in the chair next to her. "You're welcome."

Mrs. Hargrove kept the smile on her face. She was glad Charley could remember what they were supposed to be doing here. For a moment, back there in the doorway, she'd completely forgotten why Charley was wiping away the tear that was rolling down her cheek. The tear had come from her discouragement and Charley had given a convincing performance. He'd almost had her believing he felt the kind of tenderness for her that a man felt for a woman he loved.

"You'll need to sign up for the next pageant the town does," Mrs. Hargrove said, leaning over to Charley. "I never knew you had so much stage talent."

Charley grunted as he looked up.

Doris June had walked over to the table by now and pulled out a chair next to the one her mother sat in. That left Curt to share the far side of the table with Ben.

"Who has stage talent?" Curt asked as he looked around the table.

Lucy had gone back to the kitchen to get some menus. She was bringing them over to the table now.

"Everyone in your family has talent." Mrs. Hargrove didn't want to call attention to Charley's performance. "I bet Ben is good with that guitar of his."

"He plays wonderfully," Lucy said as she handed out the menus. "And he can sing, too."

"He can?" Charley asked as he took one of the menus from Lucy. "I've never heard him sing."

"The two of you will have to do a duet," Mrs. Hargrove said. "We'd love to hear you perform."

Ben took a sudden interest in the menu.

"Oh, we already have some performance plans in the works," Lucy said with confidence. "We're putting together an outdoor concert with some other kids. Linda said we could use her portable sound system and we're hoping to use a pickup truck for the stage. We have a Web site and everything."

"Why, I had no idea." Mrs. Hargrove wondered if all of the Nelson men were so closemouthed about their talents. "A concert sounds wonderful."

DORIS JUNE TRIED to discreetly step on Curt's toe. They were not sitting next to each other at the table, but she could estimate where his toe would be and she wanted to call his attention to their parents without saying anything aloud to alert them. She hadn't missed the dreamy-eyed look on her mother's face as she was glancing over at Charley and talking about talent.

Of course, if Doris June wasn't worried that her mother might be suffering from senior confusion, she wouldn't have the nerve to interfere in her mother's love life. It's just that she couldn't believe her mother even had a love life. Her mother had never seemed to notice any man, at least not after Doris June's father had died. Her mother had been good friends with Charley Nelson for decades, but that couldn't mean anything. Besides, Doris June didn't want to see the two of them lose that friendship just because one or the other of them had an episode of confusion and thought they had romantic feelings for the other.

Doris June knew the line between friendship and love could be fuzzy and it wasn't so easy to cross back and forth. What if her mother only imagined she felt something romantic for Charley, or what if she only imagined he felt something for her? Doris June knew her mother would be very sad if she lost Charley's friendship.

Doris June decided she must have pressed against the top of Curt's shoe a little too hard. She got his attention, but it was in the form of a scowl. Still, she didn't let that stop her. She nodded toward her mother so Curt would take note of the expression in her mother's eyes as her mother looked over at his father.

Curt looked and then looked back at Doris June, a frown accompanying his scowl. Doris June was glad to see he didn't look any too happy about what was happening between their parents, either.

"Does anyone want to hear the specials?" Lucy offered. She'd been waiting patiently for their order.

"I think we'll just have pie, dear," Mrs. Hargrove said as she looked around the table.

"Cherry or lemon meringue?" Lucy said as a phone rang in the kitchen.

"Can you heat the cherry pie up and add a scoop of vanilla ice cream?" Charley asked.

Lucy nodded.

"Then, that will do it for me."

Doris June wanted lemon meringue, but everyone else chose cherry.

"Not that we should be ordering pie in a restaurant when your mother can bake any kind of pie known to man," Charley said to Doris June. "She's a marvel in the kitchen."

"She hasn't been cooking much lately," Doris June said. She hoped it wasn't Charley who was pretending to be interested in her mother just because she could fry him up liver and onions whenever he wanted.

Her mother deserved someone who appreciated her for more than her cooking skills. "Usually she eats cold cereal and canned soup."

"Well, only when I'm alone, dear," Mrs. Hargrove said to Doris June. "Now that you're here, I'll certainly do more cooking. And I always enjoy your cooking, too." Mrs. Hargrove smiled at Curt. "Doris June is a wonderful cook. She makes that lasagna you like even better than I do."

Doris June groaned. Fortunately, no one heard her because Linda had come to the table with a cordless phone in her hand.

"It's the state," Linda whispered to Charley and Mrs. Hargrove. "Some guy wondering how you're coming along with the write-up for the tourism board. I tried to stall him, but he has questions. We're going to get an official Dry Creek telephone number so the calls don't always end up at the café. I don't know what to tell him. He says he's in Billings today, but he wants to drive over to Dry Creek tomorrow late afternoon and meet with you to see if he can help. Something about the students and class schedules and moving the deadlines."

"Oh," Mrs. Hargrove said.

"Oh, no," Charley echoed.

There was a moment of silence.

"Well, he can't come here," Mrs. Hargrove finally said. "We're not ready for him. Besides, no one said anything about someone coming here. We were just supposed to send in the form."

"I can help you with the form, if you haven't finished it," Doris June offered. She didn't like to see her mother so flustered.

"No." Charley shook his head.

Doris June saw her mother look around in panic and was going to say something to reassure her when Charley reached over and put his hand over her mother's hand. Doris June noticed her mother calmed right down.

"We'll figure out what to do about the state guy," Charley said.

"He said he'd be here at four o'clock tomorrow," Linda said as she held out the phone to Charley. "Why don't you talk to him?"

"I guess we should see what he has to say." Charley took the phone from Linda and put it up to his ear.

Charley only said a few words here and there, but Doris June knew he wasn't hearing good news.

"He's determined to come here tomorrow," Charley said, after he hung up from his call and gave the phone back to Linda. "Said he's always wanted to have a look around the town of Dry Creek anyway. Wants to see where the—you know." Charley looked meaningfully at Mrs. Hargrove. "Anyway, he wants to make sure it's still standing."

Doris June wanted to reassure her mother and Charley. Fortunately, she could do that with the truth. "That shouldn't be a problem. All of the buildings in Dry Creek are standing, especially after someone fixed up that one old building and made it into a dance studio. It was the only building that needed attention."

Doris June looked at everyone around the table. Curt looked as bewildered as she felt so he must not know what their parents were worried about, either. Ben didn't seem to know anything. Only Linda looked at Doris June with sympathy in her eyes before she headed back to the kitchen.

"It's not a building," Charley finally said as he looked over at Mrs. Hargrove. "I think we need to tell them. The news will be all over town tomorrow anyway when the state guy gets here."

Doris June heard her mother take a deep breath.

"It's the stop sign, dear."

Doris June thought she had heard wrong. "The what?"

"You know," her mother repeated. "The stop sign."

There was silence for a moment.

"You mean *that* stop sign?" Curt asked.

"What could anyone possibly want with *that* stop sign?" Doris June asked. She hoped this was all some kind of a mix-up.

"The old sign that's shaped like a heart?" Ben asked quietly.

Mrs. Hargrove and Charley both nodded their heads.

"They want to feature the sign in their Montana tourist book," Mrs. Hargrove said.

"One-Stop-Sign Towns," Charley added. "It's some new gimmick to get people to visit the state."

Doris June would have a question or two to ask the tourism guy if he did show up tomorrow. She might not be paying taxes in Montana, but her mother was. Surely they had better ideas than this.

"I can't believe people would come to see a stop sign," Curt said. "What happened to the parks? I thought Glacier and Yellowstone were enough to bring people to Montana."

"Well, they're both in the west," Charley said. "This guide book is for southeastern Montana."

"We have Custer's battlefield," Curt said. "That should be enough."

Doris June just sat there. She finally realized why her mother had been acting so strange lately. Her mother knew how they would all feel about seeing the stop sign used in some guidebook. No wonder her mother had been all teary eyed and confused. It had nothing to do with senility or newly discovered love. "What are we going to do?"

Doris June saw her mother and Charley exchange glances. No one even noticed that Lucy had come back with their slices of pie and was setting the plates in front of everyone.

"We were hoping to get the tourism board all excited about the pansies we're growing for Mother's Day," Mrs. Hargrove finally said. "We thought they might like that better than the old stop sign."

"Maybe we could find a field of Montana wildflowers, too," Doris June said. "People always love flowers. Look at Holland and their tulips."

"Someone should take the sign down," Curt said. "It's a nuisance. Should have been brought down years ago."

"It's state property," Charley cautioned.

"I'm willing to pay whatever fine there is for removing it," Curt said. "Besides, no one stops at that intersection anyway. Dry Creek doesn't need the sign."

"We need it for our concert," Ben said quietly.

Everyone was silent.

"You're not talking about *that* sign, are you?" Lucy said as she put the last slice of pie on the table. She looked aghast. "That sign's a landmark."

"What do you mean you need it for your concert?" Curt asked.

"That's where we're holding the concert," Lucy explained. "We're doing old love ballads at the broken-heart sign. It's our theme. We've got the Web site and we've already made flyers. We might even get extra credit for the concert at school if Mr. Jenkins will okay it."

Lucy pointed to the bulletin board just inside the café and, sure enough, Doris June saw a yellow flyer there with a drawing that resembled the old stop sign.

"Wouldn't it be better to hold your concert in the theatre?" Mrs. Hargrove suggested. "It's so much more comfortable there. There would be enough pews for a lot of people."

"We don't need seats. We plan to sit on

the grass," Lucy said. "You can't have an outdoor concert inside a theatre."

"Besides, we need the sign for our theme," Ben added as he looked at his father. "It's all about love and broken hearts and—"

Curt sighed. Doris June knew Curt was going to give in even before he cleared his throat. "When are you planning to hold this concert?"

"This Saturday night."

"The night before Mother's Day?" Mrs. Hargrove asked.

Ben nodded. "Lucy and I don't have to worry about Mother's Day."

Doris June knew that if Curt didn't fold on that remark, she would fold on his behalf. Lucy's mother had died years ago and Ben's might as well have. "I don't think it would hurt to wait until after Mother's Day to do something about the sign."

"So we can have our concert?" Lucy asked.

Curt looked at Doris June and she looked right back at him. She wondered if he was remembering what it felt like to be fifteen.

They both looked up at the two teenagers and nodded.

"You won't regret it," Lucy promised.

"See that we don't," Curt said. "I'm sure you've planned to have some adults at the concert to see there's no alcohol or drugs."

Lucy and Ben stared at him blankly.

"Well, you have four adults now," Curt said as he looked around the table. "Make sure kids know when you invite them that it'll be supervised. No alcohol. No drugs. If we see anyone with something, we call the police."

"You won't walk around or anything, will you?" Ben asked anxiously.

"Not if everything goes by the rules," Curt agreed. "We'll watch from the corners."

"Okay." Ben nodded and then asked, "Maybe you could sit in the old pickup during the performance."

Curt looked at his son. "What old pickup?"

"Ben said you still have the old pickup out in one of the barns at your place," Lucy finally said. "You know, the one that hit the sign. We thought it would make a great stage."

"We need a place for the performers," Ben added. "Those old pickups are big in the back."

"I doubt the old thing even runs anymore," Curt said.

"We could pull it into town with Grandpa's tractor," Ben suggested. "Please."

Curt nodded in defeat. "But when the concert's over, that sign's coming down."

Doris June wondered if the man from the tourism board would accept the fact that the sign he was interested in was still standing but that it wouldn't be standing long enough to make it a tourist attraction.

"You're sure you're okay with all this concert business?" Curt turned to Doris June and asked.

She nodded. She couldn't say no to the looks on the faces of Ben and Lucy.

"Well, it's only a sign," Curt finally agreed. "One stubborn piece of metal sticking out of the ground."

"I'm sure the highway department will agree to let us take it down eventually anyway. It's a menace leaving the thing up," Doris June said. "Maybe the guy from the state will pass word along to the highway department that someone needs to do something about the sign."

Doris June decided her mother was finally looking like her old self again.

"I don't know why we fretted so much about telling you about the tourism board wanting to use that sign," Mrs. Hargrove said.

"The two of you always have a mature view of things," Charley added. "We should have taken that into account."

Doris June didn't answer that remark. No one had thought they were mature twenty-five years ago.

"Maybe if we tear down the sign, we can let bygones be bygones and be friends again," Curt said, looking directly at Doris June. "I know I'm sorry for the way things turned out."

Doris June wasn't quite ready for that yet. She had heard Curt earlier when he mumbled something about being sorry for what he had done, but she hadn't expected him to apologize again so openly in front of everyone like this. "I'm sorry, too."

If Curt noticed that she hadn't directly accepted his apology, he didn't give any indication of it. He just nodded his head at her as if her words settled everything. She wished they could settle it. It made her feel small that she couldn't forgive someone for hurting her twenty-five years ago.

Maybe she could release some of her bitterness toward Curt. After all, it wasn't all his fault that she'd never married and had children. She certainly could have married someone else. She had known after he got married that there was no point in waiting for him. She'd put him out of her mind as best as she could. It was just that she had never met a man who compared to the Curt of her youth.

Doris June looked over at Curt now as he ate his cherry pie. He didn't look all that different from other men. It must have just been that she knew him so well. He had been her childhood friend. What other man could compete with that? He had been her best friend.

CHAPTER SEVEN

THE SUN WAS beginning to rise the next morning when Doris June woke up with a headache. Before she had gone to bed last night, her mother had shown her the forms that needed to be filled out for the tourism board. The letter that accompanied the forms said a Mr. Aaron White was very pleased to include Dry Creek in their tourism publication this year. He said they expected to distribute fifty thousand copies of the guide and that it was being put together as a special project by students in high schools throughout the Billings area.

When Doris June read about the high school students who were designing the tourism guide, she knew why it would have been impossible for her mother to simply decline the offer to be part of the guide. Her mother always supported education for children and teenagers.

Her mother probably hadn't even thought past the education aspect to what it would mean for Dry Creek to be included in the tourism guide, but Doris June saw the benefits immediately. Even if two percent of the people who received the guide came to Dry Creek, that would be one thousand new visitors. That should probably translate to an additional one thousand cheeseburger platters sold in Linda's café. That alone could mean a college fund for Lucy, especially if the visitors ordered pie with their cheeseburgers.

And then, after eating their cheeseburgers, those same people would likely wander over to the hardware store and some of them might buy one of the paintings Glory Becker had for sale. Glory had been saving for a trip to England. A few paintings might make a difference in her going.

And, then, if any of the visitors came late in the day, they might even want to rent the room over the garage that her mother had fixed up like a hotel room for the stray traveler who wanted to stay overnight in

Dry Creek. Her mother could use the extra income that would bring.

Doris June had never translated her resentments into cold, hard cash before but she had to wonder if her embarrassment at seeing a picture of the old stop sign on a travel guide was worth all of the money others would lose if they weren't included in the guide.

If they could not find something else to tempt the tourism board, Doris June knew she had to force herself to be okay with the proposed stop-sign angle. If that old piece of metal could ring up some dollars on the cash registers around town, then she would just have to make her peace with it. She was a grown woman and she could do it.

Doris June could smell the coffee brewing as she went down the steps to the kitchen. She expected to see her mother in her bathrobe at this hour, but Mrs. Hargrove had on a gingham housedress and a sweater. The light over the kitchen sink was on and her mother was packing the wicker picnic basket they had used in the summers on the farm.

"Oh, good, you're up," her mother said as she looked up from the basket. "Are you feeling okay this morning? I'm sorry about last night and all the fuss about the sign."

"It's barely six o'clock. What are you doing up at this hour?"

"I couldn't sleep," Mrs. Hargrove said.

"You shouldn't worry about that guide." Doris June walked over and gave her mother a hug. "However things turn out with that old sign, they will be okay. Really, it's just an old piece of metal and if people want to come here to see it, we'll let them."

Doris June felt her mother quiver.

"It's more than the sign. I've blamed myself for years for not handling things better all those years ago," Mrs. Hargrove said as she put the lid down on the wicker basket. "I did tell you how many times Curt asked for your address, didn't I? And how your father and I decided not to give it to him? We didn't mean we'd never give it to him. It was just supposed to be until you finished high school. None of us thought he'd go sign up for the army and leave town."

Doris June nodded. "I know. It was just one of those things."

Mrs. Hargrove's voice was shaky. "I never meant to make you unhappy."

"It was a long time ago," Doris June said as she gave her mother's shoulders a final squeeze. "I made my choices, too. It's okay."

Her mother gave Doris June a hug in return. "I worry about you way up there in Alaska."

"Well, I worry about you, too."

"Me?" Her mother looked up in surprise. "Why would you worry about me? I'm here at home."

That was the difference, Doris June thought to herself. Dry Creek would always be home for both of them. It had not seemed like a big enough place for Doris June to live her life when she was young, but now that she'd been other places, she thought she could come back home and be content to stay. She didn't want to say anything to her mother, however, until she had time to think about it.

She knew if she was going to live here,

she needed to make her peace with more than the stop sign. She needed to be able to see Curt and have no feelings for him whatsoever, except possibly the same sort of mild affection she had for his father or for any of the other old men who always seemed to hang around the hardware store in Dry Creek.

Doris June straightened her shoulders. She didn't need to make the whole thing seem harder than it was. For all she knew, once she got over the awkwardness of how she and Curt had parted, maybe all that would be left was that sort of mild affection. She needed to remember that she hadn't spent any time with Curt for years. Most likely the intense feelings she used to have for him were so dried out that they would crumble the first time they had any kind of a disagreement.

In the meantime, Doris June didn't plan to sit around and waste the day worrying about Curt.

"After breakfast, we should drive out to see your pansies," Doris June said. "The man from the tourism board won't be here until later today."

"I was thinking that, as long as we're up so early and we're going out to the farm anyway, we could take breakfast to Ben," Mrs. Hargrove said. "I heard the poor boy has never had homemade French toast. They just get that frozen kind that you pop up in a toaster. Whoever heard of pop-up French toast?"

Doris June smiled. Her mother never could resist a hungry child, especially a motherless one. Now that Doris June had made her decision to get past her awkward feelings with Curt, she decided she might as well start now. "If you think they're up, we should take breakfast for everyone."

"Oh, they're up all right. They keep farm hours. They have to eat breakfast early so Ben can do his chores and catch the school bus." Mrs. Hargrove tucked a cloth napkin in the wicker basket and beamed. "Besides, it's a beautiful day."

The air was cool when Doris June and her mother stepped out of the car at the Nelson farm. It was around six-thirty in the morning and the sky was still rosy from the sunrise. The car had run fitfully all the way out to the farm and Doris June was grateful she was wearing her jeans and an old flannel shirt her mother kept around for gardening. She kept expecting she would have to walk the final miles to the Nelson farm, but her mother's car kept moving slowly along.

The air always smelled better when the ground had been plowed recently, Doris June thought as she stepped out of the car and looked at a stretch of farmland that Curt was getting ready to plant. She could almost smell the damp earth.

The Nelson farmhouse was in a slight hollow that formed a windbreak from the winter blizzards. There were a couple of pine trees that Curt's mother had planted years ago near the house. Doris June could see the black electrical wires that trailed through the branches, waiting for December to arrive so the outdoor Christmas lights could be plugged in once again.

Doris June and her mother had barely

stepped from the car when Charley came out of the house.

"I was getting worried," Charley said as he walked over to them. He had wool mufflers over his ears but no coat on his back. "After you called to say you were coming, I got to thinking about your car not doing so well. It's low enough in back it could scrape on those deep ruts we've got now when you came up the hill. Our road got all messed up in the last big rain and nobody's come out from the county to fix it yet. I need to call them again."

"You know nobody's going to come grade the road until all of the spring rains are over," Mrs. Hargrove said as she opened the car trunk and started to lift out the basket. "Here, help me carry this."

"I'll get the basket," Doris June said as she reached over and helped her mother pull it out of the trunk. "Neither one of you should be carrying heavy things around at your age."

"We're not that old," Charley protested.

Mrs. Hargrove cleared her throat.

"Although we do still need help with

those pansy baskets," Mrs. Hargrove said quickly as she gave Charley a look. To make her words even more convincing, Mrs. Hargrove took a moment to lean against the car.

Doris June grinned at them as she picked up the basket. She'd figured out by now, of course, that the two of them had wanted her to come home for reasons other than to lift some baskets around for Mother's Day, but it wouldn't hurt to use their lifting request to force them to take it a little easier. Even if they were both healthy, they really shouldn't be lifting heavy things.

Curt was in the barn when he heard the honking from the horn on his dad's car. The honking meant Mrs. Hargrove and Doris June were here and that he was invited to come to breakfast. He'd told his dad that if there was any hesitancy at all from either of the women, he would just skip breakfast and get to his plowing. He quickly finished throwing hay to the horses; he was glad he was being welcomed in for the meal.

Curt scraped his boots while he was on

the porch. He could see through the open door that Ben was already deep in the midst of cooking with Mrs. Hargrove. She was instructing him on how to dip a bread slice into the egg mixture and the look of concentration on Ben's face told Curt his son was committing every step of the process to memory.

The water in the sink just off the porch always ran a little cool, but Curt liked to wash up there rather than in the main part of the house. He kept a bar of green farmer's soap there that would wash away everything from axle grease to pine pitch. Fortunately, it also smelled fresh. He lathered his hands and forearms with soap and then dried them on the towel on the nearby rack.

Curt was rolling down his shirtsleeves as he stepped into the kitchen. "Something smells good."

"It's my French toast," Ben said proudly. "Well, mine and Mrs. Hargrove's French toast."

"You're doing all the work," Mrs. Hargrove said with an encouraging nod. "Half of making good French toast is knowing when to turn it and you've got that down just right."

"Grandpa's going to make some scrambled eggs," Ben added.

"I already put them on, the minute I heard your dad's boots on the porch," Charley said as he stood over a skillet.

Curt had to swallow for a moment. He'd forgotten what a difference it made to have a woman in the kitchen here. It was almost like his mother was still alive. He looked around. He had expected Doris June to be here, but she wasn't.

He almost asked where she was, but he figured he knew. She'd stayed back in Dry Creek. He could feel his appetite leave him. But he wouldn't let it ruin the breakfast for everyone else. He forced himself to smile. "It looks like a feast."

"And we've got cinnamon to sprinkle on the French toast," Ben said as he stepped over to the stove and scooped up the French toast that was on the skillet. He put it on the platter with the rest of the food. "And

Mrs. Hargrove said we could sprinkle a little powdered sugar on it, too."

"It's a regular party," Curt said.

"That's what Doris June said," Charley said as he walked toward the table with his scrambled eggs. "She's bringing in the potted plant from the living room to put in the middle of the table for a centerpiece."

Curt couldn't remember the last time they'd worried about having a centerpiece—or a tablecloth, for that matter. The fact that they were having both for this meal cheered him up real fast though. "You know I've been forgetting to water that plant."

"You can say that again," Doris June said as she brought the plant into the kitchen and took it over to the sink. "I've decided it needs emergency watering more than it needs to be put on the table where people are eating. I'm going to let it soak. That thing could have died in there and no one would have even noticed."

"I'm busy farming," Curt defended himself with a grin. Now, this was the Doris June he remembered. She'd spent her life in jeans, half scolding him for one thing or the other. He knew this Doris June better than the woman in a pressed suit that he'd picked up at the airport.

"What kind of a farmer is it that lets his houseplants die?" Doris June said. "You wouldn't do that if it was a stalk of wheat."

Curt just kept grinning.

Doris June sat down with everyone else at the table. She hadn't realized how much everyone was worried about her and Curt until she noticed how they all relaxed when she and Curt started to tease each other. Doris June decided she could do this thing with Curt. She would just put a blanket over her feelings and treat him as if he were Ben. Yes, she could do that. If she was lucky, no one would even notice that she was forcing it.

"Great French toast," Doris June said to Ben as she finished her first bite.

"You don't think I waited too long to flip that one?" Ben asked her. "It's kind of brown."

"Not a chance," Doris June said. "It's just crispy. My favorite."

Doris June told herself that it was an unusual event for her and her mother to come out and have breakfast with the Nelsons. If she moved back to Dry Creek, it wouldn't happen often. It was just because of the pansies and all. She didn't think she could pretend enough to do this sort of thing often, but she doubted she would need to do it more than once or twice a year. For one thing, her mother wouldn't be up all night worrying and would usually be sound asleep at this time still.

CURT KEPT LOOKING at Doris June. He was missing something and he didn't know what it was. She was acting as if she had forgiven him and that everything was okay between them. The only problem was that she'd never actually said she forgave him. She'd danced around the topic when he'd said something in front of everyone last night, but the Doris June he knew would forgive a person directly and not by implication.

He looked at her again. She sure looked like she was okay with him. Maybe she'd changed a little over the years. He was the first one to recognize that age changed the way a person related to others. They'd been teenagers the last time they'd had an argument and needed to ask forgiveness of each other. It probably wasn't fair to expect a woman in her forties to forgive someone the same way she had when she was seventeen.

And then again maybe he was just imagining the lack. Maybe she had said she forgave him and he hadn't heard it with the jumble going on in his own head. Was that even possible?

Finally, he told himself he should just accept their truce as the gift that it was. She seemed happier around him so maybe she was.

Doris June offered to do the dishes, but Charley and Mrs. Hargrove insisted that they would.

"The hot water's good for my arthritis," Mrs. Hargrove said. "And Charley doesn't mind drying, do you?"

"Not at all," Charley said with a glance at Curt. "Besides, somebody needs to take a look at that old pickup to see if the kids are going to be able to use it in their concert and you can get down and see underneath it better than I can."

Curt supposed somebody did need to see if the pickup could be driven. "The battery's probably dead. Nobody's even turned the pickup on since I've been back. How long has it been, anyway, since you've driven it?"

Charley shrugged as he picked up the empty platter from the table and started over to the counter by the sink. "I haven't had it out since you dented the fender."

"Twenty-five years!" Curt said. "You've kept it in that barn for twenty-five years."

"Cool," Ben said as he put his jacket on. "That makes it, like, what—a relic?"

"I don't think it's old enough to be a relic exactly," Doris June said.

"I sent you money to fix the fender," Curt said to his father. "I thought you at least got the thing fixed and used it to haul hay or something."

"I didn't need the pickup," Charley said as he set the platter down on the counter.

"Besides, I was saving it for when you came back. You always did like the way it took the roads around here."

"The tires have to be shot, too," Curt said as he walked over to the coatrack. They'd have to tow the old thing into Dry Creek if the kids wanted to use it as a stage for their concert.

Curt looked at Ben. "Are you sure you wouldn't just as soon have us pull one of the hay wagons into town? There'd be more room on them than the back of the pickup."

"No way," Ben said. "The pickup has history. The girls are going to go wild over it."

Curt knew his son was probably right. And, for a teenage boy, driving the girls wild was quite the temptation. He didn't think his son had ever been the center of attention like that before.

"Maybe the pickup isn't in as bad shape as you think," Charley said to Curt. Apparently Charley had noticed the look on Ben's face just like Curt had. "Why don't you take a look and see? Doris June can hold the flashlight for you while you get down to look under the engine. I remember the two of you used to work on the pickup all the time."

"Ben might want to go hold the flashlight," Doris June said as she picked up a couple of dishes from the table and started to take them to the counter.

"Yeah. Sure," Ben said.

"Ben only has a few minutes until he needs to get ready to catch the school bus," Curt said as he reached up to a shelf over the coatrack and pulled down a large metal flashlight. He turned to Doris June. "I'll need someone who can stay longer."

"Please, let's go," Ben said as he put his shoulder on the door, getting ready to open it. "If I've only got a few minutes, we'll need to look quick. When I see Lucy in school, she'll want to know if the pickup will work."

Ben looked over at Doris June and she nodded.

Curt felt his stomach relax. He figured there was as much chance that the old pickup could be fixed enough to run as there was that the pigs on the Elkton farm could fly, but if Doris June was willing to hold the flashlight, he was willing to look and see what he could do. Not that he expected it to be easy. With the old rubber in the tires and all of the belts everywhere, there was no way that vehicle would run on its own power without some major work. Of course, he could be surprised. It was an old 1950 Ford and, back then, they made pickups to last.

Curt put his hand on the door and gave it a push outward. "Well, let's get going then."

CHAPTER EIGHT

Doris June didn't really want to see the pickup, but she guessed she was going to anyway. Part of her hoped the old thing would start right up and prove that it could survive all of those years with no problem. She had spent some of the best days of her life riding around in the blue pickup. Curt had driven them to high school in Miles City many days in it. She'd thought they were so cool. The radio reception had never been particularly good, but she and Curt used to sing to the top forty songs as they came on the air.

The only light in the barn came from the open doorway they entered. Doris June looked around. The Nelsons used this barn for storage and the air inside was dusty from last fall's wheat chaff. The roof had leaked at some point and it smelled like moist dirt from the spring rains. The boards that made the walls had aged until they were gray and cracking.

"Did Grandpa really let you drive that when you were sixteen?" Ben asked after the three of them had walked over to where the pickup stood. A large tarp covered the vehicle and a couple of hay bales were stacked next to it.

"I had to have my regular license before I could drive it on the country roads," Curt said. "Just like you need to have before you drive anything alone."

Doris June knew that most of the kids around Dry Creek actually drove farm vehicles before they turned sixteen. Everyone expected them to drive because of the farm work they did. They were just not allowed to officially drive in any kind of a traffic area, not even the county roads.

"We were foolish to think of taking it to Vegas, though," Doris June added for Ben's benefit. "Even when you do get your license, you need to let your Dad know before you take any long trips."

"But my dad didn't—" Ben started.

"We got into an accident before we even

got through Dry Creek," Curt said as he put a hand on his son's shoulder. "Trust me. You don't want to do what we did."

Ben nodded. "I suppose not, but it's still kind of cool."

Curt only grunted as he walked over and reached for the faded tarp that covered the front of the pickup. "Can somebody get the other side of this?"

Ben and Doris June both went to the side of the tarp, which covered the back end of the pickup.

"Let's all lift together," Curt said.

A flurry of wheat dust came off the tarp as they lifted it up. Ben sneezed. Doris June felt dust settle on her hair, but she didn't shake it off. She was back on the farm and it felt good.

"Well, there she is," Curt said as they folded back the tarp and stood, looking at the vehicle.

"I remember it being bigger," Doris June said as she studied it. This pickup used to hold her entire world. Now, the blue paint was faded and there was a crack in the windshield on the corner of the driver's side. The light coming in through the open door kept the vehicle in shadows, but she could still see the full size of it.

"Did we put the crack in the windshield, too?" Doris June asked Curt as she saw him lay down his side of the tarp and start to walk around to the back side of the pickup.

Curt needed to squeeze close to some hay bales to walk around the vehicle.

"I'm surprised your dad didn't have the insurance replace that windshield," Doris June said.

"What insurance?" Curt reached in to open the passenger door. "He didn't carry comprehensive. He must have had liability, but that was all."

"Oh, you should always have comprehensive insurance. I can't believe we didn't make sure we had insurance. I mean, we were going to Las Vegas. There would have been all kinds of traffic there."

Doris June didn't notice until then that Ben had followed his father around the side of the pickup.

"Wow," Ben said. "You can still see

where the pickup hit the sign. It's all smashed up. You must have been going sixty miles an hour."

"Oh, I am sure we weren't going any-where near that fast," Doris June said as she walked to the driver's side and reached over to open the door. "We were still in Dry Creek. We'd have been going over the speed limit if we were going that fast."

"Which no one should ever do," Curt added as he looked down at his son. "Those speed limits are there for your own safety."

"But you wouldn't have hit the stop sign if you'd been going slower," Ben persisted.

Doris June opened the door to the driv-er's side. If she didn't know better she would swear she could still smell the af-tershave lotion Curt had worn back then. It was probably still in the fabric of the seat cushion; it smelled like fresh-cut grass. She looked over at Ben. "We didn't hit the sign because we were going fast. We didn't see the sign."

"But the sign's right there on the side of the road," Ben said. "You would have seen it unless—" Ben stopped and his face got red.

"Yeah," Curt said as he put a hand on his son's shoulder. "You should never kiss a girl when you're driving, either." Curt looked over at Doris June. "It tends to be distracting."

Doris June wasn't sure she approved of the twinkle in Curt's eye.

"Maybe you should say something about safe driving at this concert you're giving," Doris June said to change the subject. "We could get the sheriff to say a few words."

"At our concert?" Ben asked in dismay. "The sheriff?"

Curt laughed as he looked over at Doris June. "I think she's teasing you, son."

Ben nodded his head in relief. "Oh, good."

Doris couldn't quite smile back at Curt, so she smiled at Ben instead. "Of course, I'm teasing."

Doris June was beginning to think she could do this. She'd done pretty well with the reference to kissing. She just had to keep things light and forget who Curt was. She would pretend that she had only met him recently. And that the past between them was something that had happened to someone else in a book she had read or a movie she had seen. That should work.

"It's not going to hurt the dent to move the pickup, is it?" Ben said as he bent down to look at the fender more closely. "It's kind of a cool dent."

"We'll have to pull the pickup into town with the John Deere tractor," Curt said. "The chains will hook underneath the back so, no, it shouldn't hurt the fender."

"Good," Ben said as he stood up. "We'll want to park it so the dent shows when we're playing our music. It'll be great for the pictures. Lucy's sister is going to take pictures for us. In case people want to order posters."

Doris June wondered why her mother and Charley were worrying about their contribution to the tourism guide. They should have just asked Ben and Lucy to help. The two kids could put the town on the map if anyone could.

"Well, look at this," Curt said as he held out something he'd just pulled from the glove compartment. "We had a map."

The map was yellowed and had a brown spot or two on it, but it clearly said it was a map of the state of Nevada.

"I had forgotten," Doris June said. "We didn't even know the way to Las Vegas."

"You swore we needed to go through Livingston," Curt said. "And that's north of here."

"Well, we could have gone that way," Doris June protested. "Besides, I knew they had a dress shop in Livingston that carried wedding dresses."

"I told you they would have had wedding dresses in Vegas, too."

"But it wouldn't have been the same. I wanted a wedding dress from here."

"Cool," Ben said. He had found a piece of paper someplace and he was making notes on it with a pencil. "Did you actually get a wedding dress?"

Doris June shook her head. She remembered it all now. She'd only had her jeans and a couple of T-shirts with her and she had wanted something special to wear when she got married. She figured the dresses in Las Vegas would all be for older, more experienced women. She wanted to be wearing something she would be comfortable passing along to a daughter someday and she worried she wouldn't find anything like that in Nevada. She thought the dresses there would be too sexy and she didn't want that.

"I should have listened to you," Curt said as he stood there holding the map in his hand.

"Well, as it turned out, I didn't need a wedding dress," Doris June said brightly. She resisted the impulse to note that she had never needed a wedding dress after that either. "So it was okay."

Everybody was silent.

"Hey, it's great to see this old pickup though, isn't it?" Doris June made herself look at Curt and smile. "I can't believe your dad kept it."

Curt nodded and turned to Ben. "Don't you think you'd better get going so you aren't late for the school bus? It's after seven-thirty."

"I guess so," Ben said as he stood up from where he was studying the fender.

"I don't know why I have to go to school today when we're so busy getting ready for the concert."

"The concert's not until Saturday," Curt said. "There's plenty of time."

"Only two days," Ben protested, but he walked to the barn door and then turned around. "You'll wait to start talking to that guy from the state until Lucy and I get there, won't you? We'll get off the school bus in Dry Creek."

"It's your grandfather's meeting, but I'm sure he'll wait if he can." Curt watched his son leave the barn.

When Ben was gone, Curt started to walk around the pickup.

"Could you help me fold up the tarp?" Curt remembered that Doris June always talked best when she was busy. Even when they were hiking in the mountains, she talked more when she was picking up things along the trail. He wanted her to talk to him now.

"You know, I never realized," Curt said as he picked up one end of the tarp.

Doris June looked up at him as she picked up the opposite corner. "What?"

"I never knew what I was asking you to give up. I should have figured it out when you were so set on going to that place in Livingston to get a wedding dress."

Doris June shrugged. "All I had with me were jeans. Most women want a wedding dress."

"But you wanted one from a store close to home. It wasn't just that I was asking you to run away and marry me, I was asking you to get married someplace that wasn't home to either of us."

Doris June looked down at the tarp and Curt couldn't see her face. She used to be easier to read, as open as a sunny day. But no more.

"Lots of women get married away from their homes. It happens all the time."

"But not when they've barely turned seventeen," Curt said. "Not when they're you. You didn't want a Las Vegas wedding, did you?"

Doris June didn't answer him. She brought her end of the folded tarp to the place where he had folded his. "This should finish the tarp."

Curt let her walk out of the barn. He had poked around in their past enough for today. If he wasn't careful, she would never let him close to her again and, now that she was talking to him, he found that he wanted things to be like they used to be between them. He didn't want to settle for politeness when, maybe he could have his friend back.

Curt put the Nevada map back on the seat of the pickup. It was odd, but he swore he could smell the scent of the strawberry shampoo Doris June used to wash her hair with. It must still be in the fabric of the old seat cushion. He leaned a little closer to the seat back to be sure. Something purple caught his eye and he opened the door and pulled a rubber band from the crease in the seat. That was one of the bands Doris June had used in her ponytails.

Curt smiled to himself. He remembered he used to take the rubber bands out of her hair when he kissed her and it used to make her mad. She'd scold him while she put the band back in place and then she'd kiss him again. He wished she was mad at him for something as simple as that this time. Back then she could scold him proper. Now, it seemed, her anger at him only made her want to stay away from him.

Well, he told himself as he pushed the rubber band over his hand and onto his wrist, he would either have to make her more angry with him or less angry with him. Either one was likely to get a reaction. Once he got that reaction, he might be able to gauge what his chances were of eventually making peace.

The dishes were finished by the time Curt got back to the kitchen. Doris June was sitting at the table with her mother and Ben had changed into his school clothes.

"Don't you need to be going?" Curt said to his son. He knew Ben didn't want to leave the house when there was so much cheer in it for a change, but he couldn't let him miss school.

"Yeah," Ben said as he walked to the door. "Be sure and wait for us, Grandpa."

"I will," Charley said as Ben opened the door. "I'll tell him my jokes if I need to."

Ben groaned and walked through the door.

"Since the meeting with that fella from the state won't be until late this afternoon," Charley said as he turned to Curt, "we thought we'd go over and tend to the pansies before he gets here. Want to come?"

"Yeah, I think I would," Curt said. He should be plowing, but it would have to wait. "Let me get cleaned up some first."

"There's no need to change," Mrs. Hargrove said. "We're going to be working in dirt over there anyway."

Curt rolled down the sleeves on his work shirt. "Well, then, I'm ready to go. Just let me go get my shovel."

"Do you have an extra one for me?" Doris June asked.

Curt nodded as he left the house.

Fifteen minutes later, Doris June drove her mother's car into the yard next to their family's old farmhouse. With one thing and another, she hadn't been back to visit the farm in several years. Her mother and

Charley had both come with her in the car since Curt wanted to drive one of the small tractors over. He planned to do a little plowing when they finished doing what they needed to do with the pansies.

All the way over to the farm, the car had kept acting up and Doris June half expected she would have to walk back to the Nelson farm and borrow one of their pickups. But her mother's old car managed to get them to their farm.

Doris June took a deep breath as she stepped from the car, thinking again that the air did smell better when the ground had been plowed recently. She looked at the stretch of land that bordered the field Curt had freshly worked. He had planted part of it in wheat and she could see tiny green sprouts coming up in rows. At the side of the field was a strip of ground covered with a plastic tarp. She could see small sections of lavender through the plastic.

"We've got baskets in the old house," Mrs. Hargrove said as she got out of the car and walked over to stand beside Doris June. "The pansies are ready to go in the baskets anytime now. I thought we'd spend the day tomorrow getting the baskets ready and then Curt said he can truck them over to the town hall on Saturday."

"We've got our work cut out for us, all right," Charley said as he joined them. "What with the baskets and the concert, we'll be busy."

Charley didn't sound displeased at the prospect of work.

"Ben and Lucy might help us on Saturday," Mrs. Hargrove said. "If we help them some with the concert, they'll have time."

"I thought of asking them before," Charley said. "But I wondered—I mean, since neither one of them has a mother, at least not here, I thought the baskets might bother them."

"Oh," Mrs. Hargrove said and thought a minute. "But maybe it would make them feel better to do something for mothers in general. So they're part of everything anyway."

"Maybe." Charley shrugged. "I just don't know."

Doris June decided she was glad that

her mother and Charley had something to worry about besides the stop sign. It gave her time to walk over to the house. The house here was as much a home to her as the house where her mother now lived in Dry Creek. For years while Doris June was a child, their family had spent the summers on the farm and then moved into their Dry Creek house for the school months. There had been no school bus in those days and the roads out by the farm were often closed because of snow, so most families with schoolchildren had a place to stay in town in addition to their farmhouse.

Doris June opened the door to the old house. It was never kept locked, although it was latched tight so the wind wouldn't blow the door open in a blizzard. The light was dim as Doris June stepped inside. The windows were boarded up to keep the glass from being broken and the roof had a tarp over it that draped down to cover the cracks in the windows on the south side of the house.

As she stood in the kitchen, with the open door to her back, Doris June could hear Charley telling her mother that he was going to wait for Curt. The kitchen was obviously where they were setting up their Mother's Day production facility. There were stacks of baskets along the tile counter that ran along one side of the kitchen. The air inside the house smelled musty, but Doris June still detected the faint scent of cinnamon left from the days when her mother used to bake sweet rolls in the kitchen.

"I always miss your father when I come here," Mrs. Hargrove said as she entered the house. There was a plain Formica table in the middle of the kitchen and Mrs. Hargrove went over to it and sat in one of the chairs surrounding it. "Your father was always happiest when he could be out here."

Doris June watched as her mother crossed her arms to keep warm.

"I remember Dad plowing and getting so excited when he'd finish a field," Doris June said.

"Farming was a contest to him," Mrs. Hargrove admitted. "He liked the challenge—to see if he could beat the rain or if he could beat Charley with the plowing. Their fields were about the same size and they made a point of starting on the same day."

Doris June smiled.

"Of course, I suspected for a long time that Charley let your dad win," Mrs. Hargrove said. "Charley would always be just a little bit behind him, but he never did seem to pass him."

"You should ask Charley."

Mrs. Hargrove shook her head. "I'm not sure Charley would want me to know. It'd make him feel soft. Men don't always like that. So I let him keep his secret. I think it made Charley happy to do it. Those were good days for your father."

"Were you happy here?" Doris June asked as she sat down in one of the other chairs. She could feel the metal bars of the chair on her back. "I mean for yourself and not just because of Dad?"

Mrs. Hargrove smiled. "It took me some time to get used to the farm, but, in time, I liked the peace out here as much as your father did. When we first got married, I used to think nothing would suit me but city life. Your father and I, we were such opposites when we got married."

Doris June could remember her father well. He'd died almost twenty years ago, but he'd always seemed bigger than life. He had enough gusto for ten men. It was strange, but she didn't have as clear a picture of her mother from those days as she did of her father. Her mother had always paled in comparison to her father. It was odd to think of that now though because her mother was not at all timid these days. She had blossomed as she grew older.

"Did you think I wouldn't be happy if I'd married Curt back then?"

Mrs. Hargrove stiffened. "It wasn't Curt. I've always said you were too young."

Doris June nodded. Her mother had always said that. It wasn't until now, however, that Doris June was wondering if there hadn't been other reasons. "Were you happy when you first got married?"

Mrs. Hargrove hugged her arms and didn't answer at first. Finally, she said.

"Your father was a saint. But, sometimes, it's hard when people marry too young. For women, especially, if they don't know who they are and what they want in life. It can be hard for them to find their footing."

Doris June reached across the table and patted her mother's arm. They sat together as the morning light filtered in through the open door and the cracks in some of the boards hanging over the windows.

"I wanted you to be happy," Mrs. Hargrove finally said.

"I know." Doris June wasn't sure she had fully forgiven her mother for interfering until this very moment. In her mind, it had been her mother who stopped everything that day twenty-five years ago. Her father might have forbidden her to get married, but she didn't remember him being as adamant as her mother had been. It was odd, but in the years since then, she had never thought about why her mother had been so sure it was not good to be married young.

Looking at her mother now, Doris June knew she had to do something to relieve her mother's guilt. It was that guilt and not some sort of senior confusion that was eating away at her mother's confidence.

"I'm okay, really I am," Doris June said. "You did what any parent would do."

"Yes, but—"

"Really, I'm good," Doris June said. She heard a humming in the distance that could only be a tractor coming down the road. Doris June didn't know what else to say so she just sat with her mother. In a few minutes, she heard boots on the porch just outside of the kitchen.

"Anybody home?" Curt called out.

"We're in here," Doris June said as she stood up. "We were just going out to see the pansies."

Curt stepped into the open door of the kitchen. "Why don't you grab one of those baskets so we can see how many pansies we need to make them look full?"

"Will do." Doris June picked up a basket as she walked past the counter. She looked back at her mother. "See, everything's okay."

Mrs. Hargrove stood up and nodded. "I'll be right behind you."

Curt was already heading to the pansy patch, but he turned around and smiled when he saw Doris June walk out of the door and stand for a minute on the porch to take a deep breath of the farm air. This was the Doris June he knew. He liked seeing her in old jeans and a flannel shirt even more than he'd liked seeing her in the soft pink dress last night, and that was saying something.

"I'll pull back the plastic and we'll take a look," Curt said when Doris June got to the pansies. Charley was already standing by the flowers and Mrs. Hargrove was following along behind.

It only took Curt one motion of his arm to pull back the plastic. The plastic itself was warm because of the solar lights. He'd read the directions when he put the stuff down to be sure that it would never get hot enough to melt or to start a fire.

"They're beautiful," Doris June said as they stood and looked down at the flowers.

"They're still awfully small," Mrs. Hargrove fretted. "I wanted them to be bigger by now."

"Isn't that what all mothers say," Charley said with a smile.

"I think they're just perfect," Doris June said. "When they're small like this, we can crowd the baskets with them. It will be all lavender and purple and those bits of yellow velvet."

"We have some moss to put around the plants, too," Curt said. "That way we can water them well on Saturday and they'll be all set for giving away on Sunday morning."

"Did anyone remember to buy ribbon?" Doris June asked.

"I have lots of yellow ribbon left from when we decorated the tree in front of the town hall," Mrs. Hargrove said. "I brought that out from town the other day along with bits and pieces of other ribbon."

"Why don't you and Charley put the ribbons on the baskets while Doris June and I dig?" Curt said to Mrs. Hargrove.

"Well, I can—" Charley started to say something and then Mrs. Hargrove put her hand on his arm. He cleared his throat.

"Oh, yeah, never mind. We'll leave the hard work to you young ones."

Mrs. Hargrove and Charley walked into the farmhouse.

CURT WATCHED HIS father and Mrs. Hargrove leave and then he turned to Doris June. "We've been had, you know."

"Yeah, I figured. But they shouldn't be lifting things and digging holes even if they still think they can."

Curt nodded. "I should have brought us some hoes instead of these shovels." He looked down at the pansies. "The plants are so little. I don't want to damage them."

"We'll be careful," Doris June said.

Curt liked the rhythm he and Doris June got into. She was tense at first when they were alone so he didn't say anything. He just worked. He'd sink his shovel between the rows and she would use her shovel to lift the individual plants out of the dirt. When they had a dozen or so pansies unearthed, they put them in one of the plastic trays that sat beside the plants and started on another tray.

Curt could tell Doris June relaxed around him as they worked. He didn't want to disturb that, but he finally asked her a question about her job in Anchorage. Before he knew it, the sun was high in the sky and he knew all about what a traffic control manager did at a television station.

"You like your job, don't you?" Curt finally stopped digging and leaned on his shovel.

Doris June nodded and patted the dirt around their last tray of pansies.

"I bet everyone's getting hungry," Curt said. "It must be past one."

"We should be getting home," Doris June said. "I need to press something to wear for our meeting tonight."

"You look fine to me." Curt looked at Doris June. "There's nothing wrong with what you're wearing."

"I thought I'd change into a suit," Doris June said.

Curt had been afraid of that. He didn't know when she had become so fond of suits. "The guy from the state is probably in his twenties. He's probably going to wear cutoffs and a T-shirt."

"I wouldn't count on it. A guy in his twenties can still be wearing a suit," Doris June said as she stood up and stretched her back. "He's in business."

"He's with the state," Curt said. "Even if he's going to dress up, we don't need to impress him. We're the taxpayers."

Doris June was, of course, halfway to the house by the time he said that.

It was a good thing he had another white shirt, Curt told himself. He couldn't remember the last time he'd put a suit on twice in the same week.

CHAPTER NINE

DORIS JUNE SLID into the jacket of her navy suit and stepped in front of the mirror in her old bedroom to make sure her hair was all in place. The mirror had a black rim around it where it had aged. There was still some tape in the corner where she used to put notes to herself about school assignments.

When Doris June looked in the mirror, she could see how she had changed over the years. Some of it was good, some of it was bad. The basics were still the same. She had blond hair that was too dark to be really fashionable and eyes that were too light a blue to be mysterious. Her cheeks had always been pink and bordering on chubby. Her face looked more settled than it had when she stood at this mirror in her school days. She moved slower, but maybe she wasn't as impatient. She seemed more solid.

She didn't look as though she was as easily swayed as she had been back then. She straightened her jacket. Wearing a suit made her feel she was more in charge of her own opinions. In her youth, she'd been like a puppy, happily going this way and that way, never knowing which direction she really wanted to take.

When Curt had reminded her about their argument on what route to take to Las Vegas, she remembered how hard it had been for her to try to stand up for what she did want even when she knew what it was. She had tried to tell him that it was going to be her wedding, too, and that she wanted it to be nice.

She smoothed back her hair and added a gold pin to her suit jacket. Curt had always been the one who made the decisions for them. It had seemed exciting at sixteen, but even as they talked about eloping, some part of her had wondered if he would always insist on doing things his way.

Her mother and father had shared the decisions in their family; at least it had looked that way to her. She knew it had never done her any good to cry poor-me to either one of them. The one who hadn't made the decision always backed the one who had. It had been frustrating as a child, but she had always imagined that was what a marriage was supposed to be like. From what her mother had said this morning, though, she wondered if the balance of power had been the same at the beginning of their marriage.

"Doris June," her mother called up the stairs. "It's almost time to go."

"I'll be right down." Doris June turned away from the mirror and started toward the stairs.

The day had grown warmer as time passed, and now that it was almost four o'clock the heat of the day was pressed down and waiting as Doris June opened the door to go outside.

"No rain today," Mrs. Hargrove said as she stepped out onto her porch and followed Doris June down the steps. "It makes the ground better for walking, but the crops will need it soon."

"It'll probably rain some before long." Doris June adjusted her steps to match those of her mother. "Here take my arm. There are ruts along the road here."

Mrs. Hargrove put her hand on Doris June's arm.

"I hope you're careful when you walk along here by yourself," Doris June said as she tucked her mother's hand closer to her. "You don't want to fall."

"I'm careful," Mrs. Hargrove assured her. "You don't need to worry."

The two of them walked to the café.

"I suppose we should offer him some coffee," Mrs. Hargrove said as they climbed the steps to the café.

"I think that would be nice."

When the two women entered the café, Doris June could tell right away that the man at the table on the left was the state man even though he had an empty platter in front of him that indicated he'd eaten in the café, so he could really be anyone. If they got more visitors in Dry Creek, Doris June might not have known for sure who he was.

Curt had been right about him. He looked like he was about twenty-five. But she had been right, too. He had on a beige suit that had probably cost him a week's salary.

"Doris June Hargrove." She put her hand out to the state man as she finished walking over to his table. "You must be Mr. Aaron White."

"Yes." He stood up. "I'm Aaron. So glad you could meet me."

"My mother is the one who is writing the piece for your publication. Well, she and Charley Nelson," Doris June said as she pulled out a chair for her mother. "I'm just along for the ride."

"Well, I'm pleased to meet both of you."

"Charley Nelson is the man you talked to yesterday on the phone," Mrs. Hargrove said. "He'll be here any minute, with his son. I hope we haven't kept you waiting?"

"I got here early so I had a late lunch," Aaron said as he looked over at the kitchen door. "Linda has been filling me in on the plans the kids have for a concert here and

I'm beginning to think you don't even need the tourism guide."

Linda came out of the door to the kitchen carrying a coffeepot.

"Refill?" she asked Aaron, and then looked at Mrs. Hargrove and Doris June. "Can I get anything for either of you?"

"We just ate," Mrs. Hargrove said as Linda filled Aaron's coffee cup.

"The kids will be so excited," Linda said when she finished filling the cup. "Aaron thinks their concert will be a smashing success."

"It's got grass-roots promotion written all over it," Aaron agreed. "If we could think of an educational angle to go with it, I could promote it to the high schools in Billings."

Just then Doris June heard the school bus drive into Dry Creek.

"He thinks they should even charge," Linda said. "At least enough to cover expenses."

Aaron nodded. "I can't wait to meet Lucy and Ben."

The door to the café swung open.

"They're here now," Linda said as the two teenagers raced in.

It only took a couple of minutes for Lucy and Ben to learn everything that Aaron had been telling Linda.

"You really think you could get some kids from Billings to come?" Lucy asked.

"If we can figure out an educational angle, the kids that come can even get extra credit for it in social studies. We're doing a family-preparedness section in the high schools and we're looking for fun things they can do where they actually learn something."

Lucy and Ben were silent as they thought.

"It wouldn't even need to be that much of an educational angle." Aaron took a sip of his coffee. "Sometimes soft educational works, too—you know, something that has to do with feelings and stuff."

"It's love ballads," Lucy said. "That's feelings."

"Well, it would have to be more than that," Aaron said.

The door to the café opened and Curt

and Charley walked in. They were both wearing boots and Doris June didn't need to see them to know they were heading toward the table where everyone was sitting.

"Dad, this man is going to help us with our concert," Ben announced. "Isn't that great?"

"Yeah," Curt said as he pulled a chair out and sat down at the table.

"I'll do whatever I can," Aaron said.

"Well, if you've got a big chain, we could use another one to pull the pickup in to town. I can only find the one," Charley said as he sat down at the table, too.

"What pickup?" Aaron asked. "Did I miss something?"

"We're going to bring in the real pickup," Lucy gushed. "You know, the one that hit the sign. The fender is still bent and everything."

"I sent money to have it fixed," Curt defended himself.

"It's your pickup?" Aaron asked as he turned to Curt. His voice rose in excitement. "You're the one who was eloping?"

"Well, it was technically my father's pickup," Curt said. "But, yeah, I was the one driving it when I hit the sign. It was a complete accident."

Ben chuckled. "He was trying to kiss Doris June. That's why they hit the stop sign."

Aaron looked over at Doris June and his eyes got wide.

"That's great!" Aaron was really getting animated now. "That's a perfect message for kids. The two of you could do a thing on eloping."

"They could do a driver's education piece on why it's important to watch the road when they're driving," Ben offered.

"I don't think we need to bring driving into this," Curt said. "If we're going to have any messages at the concert it should be don't drink and don't do drugs. We shouldn't even mention eloping. Everyone's too young for that."

There was a moment's silence.

"And really we're hoping to do something on flowers for the guidebook," Mrs. Hargrove said. "I have the prettiest field of pansies a few miles north of here that you have to see."

Doris June knew her mother's pansies didn't stand a chance once she saw the light in Aaron's eyes. He was an advertising person in pursuit of a new concept.

"They give out baskets of pansies to every mother who comes to the town hall Mother's Day celebrations on Sunday morning." Doris June had to try anyway. "I think we could get some local news coverage of that. Human interest stories and all."

"But the bent-heart concert could go regional," Aaron said. "I could see them picking up a news story about something like this in Denver. Maybe even Salt Lake City. It's got all the elements. Local teenagers fall in love and wreck a sign on their way to get married. Years later, their son sings love songs at the—"

"Oh, no," Doris June interrupted him. He was getting it all wrong. "We never got married. The elopement was called off."

"I know, but I thought you got married later. I mean—" Aaron looked around in bewilderment. "Well, then who's Ben's mother?"

"She's away," Doris June said. She was glad she'd worn the suit. She felt as if she was talking about someone else. "I'm not Ben's mother. His father married someone else."

"Well, that doesn't make the story nearly as good," Aaron said.

"But, it happens to be life," Curt said.

"Anyway, about those flowers," Mrs. Hargrove added gamely. "We can take you out to see them if you want."

Doris June could see out of the corner of her eye that Ben's face was bright red. He was probably wishing—as sincerely as she was—this whole thing had never happened.

"You know—" Aaron was tapping his finger on the side of his head "—it's actually better this way."

"Better for who?" Curt asked.

"Better as an educational message to go with the concert," Aaron said. "You're right, you know. It *is* how life happens. Boy doesn't always get girl. The eloping couple doesn't always get married. This could really be a good message for the kids. I could take this to the schools and call it a mental health event. Kids might even get double credit for coming."

Lucy let out a squeal and kissed Ben on the cheek. "We're going to have so many kids at our concert."

In the end, Aaron decided they might want to use the pansies as a secondary draw in the tourism guide. He said it was always good to have several listings for an area and he thought the pansies could be a small footnote in the guide.

"A small footnote?" Mrs. Hargrove muttered as they walked out of the café. "They should get more than a footnote, especially when it's only an old piece of metal that is taking first place."

"The stop sign is not taking first place," Doris June said firmly. "It's the concert the kids are giving that will be the event. The stop sign is just a stage decoration."

"It's a hazard is what it is," Curt said as he walked beside Aaron. "As a state official, you probably want to report it to the highway maintenance department. They should replace it. Or just do away with it."

"Let's walk by and see it," Aaron said as he stepped off the café porch. "I haven't had a chance to see it yet. Isn't that the sign that inspired that song by Duane Enger, the Jazz Man? You know, he's really famous these days."

"My sister used to date him," Lucy said proudly as she turned to lead the way to the sign. "Before he was famous, of course."

"Really? He lived around here?"

Lucy nodded. "He owned the café with my sister."

"Really?" Aaron turned around and looked back. "The one where I just ate? We could put a sign up. That might be a stop on the tourist trail."

"Jazz used to sing to the customers while my sister served them spaghetti dinners," Lucy added. "She makes a great spaghetti sauce. They had a special going. It was the only thing the café served."

"Don't forget about Custer's Last Stand." Curt was leading the way down the road.

"You know that's around here, too. Men died in that battle."

"Oh, but that's in all of the guidebooks," Aaron said. "Our book is about the offbeat stuff, you know, the little stuff that no one knows is in places. Local color."

"Well, if you're looking for color, Edith's pansies are the prettiest color you'll see anywhere around," Charley said. It took him a minute to realize no one had noticed he'd called Mrs. Hargrove by her given name. Of course, that might be because it looked like there was an argument brewing.

"I don't know what the point is of having a tourism guidebook if you don't guide the people to the important stuff," Curt said. "You're just giving them things that they could find in their own backyard."

"Not anymore, they can't," Aaron said. "You don't realize how unique small towns like Dry Creek are. Most people live in urban areas where no one would remember the history of a stop sign."

"Lucky them," Curt muttered. "I'm not

so sure there's any reason to remember the history of this one."

Doris June never did understand how Aaron got them all to agree to do an educational panel to go with the concert. They were standing beside the old stop sign and she had been bending down to read some of the initials carved on the post. When she looked up, Aaron was scribbling some notes on a piece of paper he'd pulled from somewhere.

"We'll want to give kids a chance to ask questions," Aaron said as he stopped writing. "That's part of what makes something like this an educational event."

"I don't know about fielding questions," Curt said as he scowled at the sign. "Would you look at the rust on that thing? It's definitely a hazard so close to the road. People shouldn't be around the thing without a tetanus shot."

The stop sign tilted a little to the left and would have fallen down years ago except for the pile of small stones that surrounded it. Someone had pulled the weeds away from the stones so the sign stood out on the shoulder of the road. There was a wide space behind the sign.

"Maybe you could tell the kids about the map," Ben suggested as he looked around the area. "About how you almost went the wrong way just because you were looking for a wedding dress."

"You almost went the wrong way?" Aaron said gleefully as he jotted down a note. "That's great. What a metaphor. Yes, we'll definitely have to talk about going the wrong way."

"I don't think the kids today will relate," Doris June said as she moved a little closer to Aaron so he could hear her. "I mean, when they see us, they'll just see their parents and—"

"But that's why it's great," Aaron said. "It will be intergenerational. The school boards love buzz words like that. Helping families relate. It's great."

Doris June hoped Aaron could see that the families standing around the stop sign didn't look like they wanted to relate, at least not in front of dozens of teenagers they didn't know.

"I never knew that someone tried to put a hole in the sign," Doris June said as she looked at the sign more carefully. Two dents had been smashed in the *o* of the "Stop." "Who would do that—mess up our sign?"

"Me," Curt said, and cleared his throat. "I did that. It was wrong, of course. But I took a rock to it before I left for the army."

"This is great," Aaron said as he made some more notes. "Anger management."

"I wouldn't recommend kids do something like that, of course," Curt said with a note of alarm. "It's defacing public property."

There was a moment's silence while Aaron made more notes.

"I hope no one asks questions about those dents," Curt muttered.

"Maybe I could make the kids some cookies," Mrs. Hargrove said. "Kids never ask as many questions when they have something to eat."

"Sounds like a plan to me," Curt said. "I could make them some pancakes."

"You think it'll last until breakfast?" Ben

asked in awe. "Wouldn't that be something? We'd be making history. The concert at the fair in Great Falls doesn't even last until breakfast."

"No, your concert won't last past midnight," Curt said. "Remember, it will be supervised."

"Oh, yeah," Ben said, but he didn't seem too disappointed. "We probably don't have enough songs ready anyway to play all night. We're going to have to repeat as it is." Ben looked around. "I don't suppose anyone else here would want to sing a number. Maybe a favorite song or something?"

"I don't sing," Curt said.

Doris June wondered if she should ask Curt to drive her into Miles City so she could buy more sugar and flour. She'd just remembered why one set of those initials carved on the stop post looked familiar. It said "D.J.H. + C.N." She'd left it as a message for Curt on her first visit home. He was in the army by then, but she knew he'd be back to visit his family. She'd thought he'd go look at the sign like she had. He must not have and she certainly didn't want him, or anyone else, to start looking now. If cookies were what it would take to discourage the kids from studying the old stop sign, then cookies they would have in an abundance.

For the first time since she'd been home, Doris June wondered if her mother could possibly still be upset that she didn't have any grandchildren. Sometimes children could ask too many questions. The only good thing about all of this was that Curt didn't look any happier at the prospect of talking about their encounter with the old stop sign than she was.

CHAPTER TEN

DORIS JUNE DROVE her mother out to the farmhouse just before dark so they could be sure the plastic covered all the pansies that were still in the ground. Doris June brought a huge basket of pansies back with them. If they were going to have to worry about what to say to teenagers at that concert and figure out how to get the flower baskets ready for Mother's Day at the same time, they deserved to have a nice centerpiece for their table.

After Doris June set the pansy basket on the table, she went into the kitchen to put some water on for tea.

"Are you going to do what Aaron wants and dress up in the clothes you wore that night?" Mrs. Hargrove asked as she sat at the table in the dining room. "I think there are a few of your old clothes in the attic, although I cut some of them up for rags over the years. I guess maybe I shouldn't have."

"I don't think I would still fit in those clothes anyway," Doris June said as she brought two cups back and set them on the table. "I used to wear a size eight. Now I'm a twelve."

"I bet your old sweaters would still fit though. You used to wear them so baggy. I don't know why you wore them that way."

"That was the style, Mother." Doris June went back to the kitchen.

"The kids might like to see what you wore back then, though," Mrs. Hargrove said. "You know, for the sake of history."

"It hasn't been that long," Doris June protested as she brought the teapot into the dining room and carefully set it on a trivet on the table. "It's not like we lived in the pioneer days."

"Kids always think anyone who's an adult lived with the dinosaurs, especially when it comes to fashion. They have no concept of how fast time goes by. To them, it's all history."

"You know, I do have the old bag I made

out of quilt blocks—the one I used as a suitcase when we were going to Vegas. I saw it on a shelf in my closet here." Doris June stopped to think a minute before she poured two cups of herbal tea and slid one cup toward her mother. "I wonder if I could interest the girls in the pattern for making the bag. That might take up some of the time we're supposed to talk. Besides, it would be educational. Who knows what they're learning in Home Economics these days."

Mrs. Hargrove cleared her throat. "I don't think they still have a Home Economics class in the high school. They're more into computers now."

"Well, all the more reason for someone to tell them a little bit about how to sew up something for themselves." Doris June sat down at the table. "They probably don't even know how to make a pattern for a bag like mine. How will they know these things if no one tells them anything?"

Mrs. Hargrove nodded as she picked up her teacup. "That's why I always feel education is so important."

Doris June and her mother drank their tea together peacefully. The more they talked about the concert on Saturday night and the pansy presentation on Sunday morning, the more they both felt that it would all work out just fine. Besides, they both decided, there were still two days to get everything ready and the kids were going to do most of the work for the concert.

When Mrs. Hargrove woke up the next morning, she felt better than she had for months. Now that she'd been able to voice some of her feelings about what had happened when Doris June and Curt had tried to elope, she was starting to feel better.

It was true that confession did a world of good for a person, she thought to herself as she swung her legs out of bed, even though really it wasn't as if there was anything for her to confess. Her actions had been right there in the open for anyone to see. It wasn't so much that she had made a mistake as it was that there was no perfect way to resolve the situation.

Love was a funny thing, Mrs. Hargrove

thought to herself as she stood up and reached for her robe. Love sometimes grew and sometimes it died. Sometimes, it even came back to life after everyone thought it was long dead.

Mrs. Hargrove hummed to herself as she walked down the hall to the bathroom. Yes, indeed, love sometimes did come back to life. She wondered when her daughter and Curt were going to realize that fact.

Mrs. Hargrove looked out the bathroom window as she washed her face. The sun was just beginning to rise and it promised to be a clear day. It would be a good day for getting the pansies ready for their baskets. Charley had already said he and Curt would be over at the Hargrove farm today if the weather was good. That meant she should be there with Doris June, too.

Mrs. Hargrove thought it would be easy enough to get her daughter out to the old farm place so they could work with the pansies. However, her daughter had another mission in mind.

"We need to make arrangements for the cookies first," Doris June said as she stood at the foot of the stairs in her jeans and an old sweatshirt with a grease stain on its sleeve. "It'll be too late when we get home from all that digging and tomorrow will be a whirlwind."

"Well, there's always time to bake cookies," Mrs. Hargrove said as she opened the closet at the bottom of the stairs and started pushing things aside. Finally, she found what she was looking for. "Don't you think this sweater would be better than that? You've got a stain all over your sleeve."

Doris June frowned at the rose-colored sweater her mother held up. "Isn't that the sweater you wear sometimes?"

"Yes, but it would look nice on you," Mrs. Hargrove said as she held it out to her daughter. "Pink's such a pretty color on you. I realized it the other night when you had that dress on."

"That dress was a disaster," Doris June said as she pushed the sleeves up on the old sweatshirt. "There, the stain isn't so bad anymore. Besides, I'm just going to get dirty anyway if we're digging in the pansies."

"It doesn't hurt for a woman to look her best even when she's working in the dirt," Mrs. Hargrove said as she kept holding out the sweater.

"Oh, I see," Doris June finally said after a second. "You're worried about me making some kind of an impression on Curt, but you don't need to be."

"I don't?" Mrs. Hargrove's eyes brightened.

"Of course not," Doris June said. "We're working together on this, but that's all. We're doing a few things to benefit Dry Creek, but that's the end of the story. Curt is just doing his civic duty."

"Oh, I don't know," Mrs. Hargrove said. "I thought he looked like he might want to—you know—get back together again."

Doris June shook her head. "Now, why would you think that? See, that's why we shouldn't do all this talking at the concert. People around here leap to funny conclusions. They see something and they think it means something more than it does."

"Yes, but sometimes—"

"No, Mother." Doris June shook her

head again. "I'm not going to get myself all worked up over something that isn't going to happen. Curt and I used to have a future. That future's long gone, though. It doesn't matter if the kids are putting on some nostalgic concert about love. All Curt and I have to look forward to is getting the pansies dug up."

Mrs. Hargrove didn't say anything more to her daughter as she hung the sweater back up in the closet, but she figured her daughter and Curt had more of a future than that. The fact was, the two of them probably had a longer future than that with the state guy, Aaron. The concert Friday night was going to be the beginning of something and not the end. Mrs. Hargrove knew teenagers well enough to know they'd see to that. Doris June and Curt would be tied to each other because of the stop sign whether they wanted to be or not.

Doris June left the house while her mother made some phone calls. She always liked to walk around Dry Creek in the morning while people were getting up for the day, so she was glad to have some time to do so. The early morning air was cool and there was enough dew on the ground to make everything a little slippery. There was a morning haze that hid the top of the Big Sheep Mountains in the north. Most of the houses had lights on in their kitchens.

Everything was still quiet, though. Doris June missed quiet like this when she went for a walk in Anchorage. Not that Anchorage in the winter wasn't quiet; it's just that the days were too cold to walk for long at that time of year and she didn't enjoy the darkness of the winter months so she was seldom out in it.

All of the lights were on in the café, so Doris June decided to go inside and have a cup of coffee. She opened the door and saw that the tables were all pushed to the side. The chairs were sitting on top of the tables like they'd been put up so someone could mop the linoleum floor.

"Linda?" Doris June called out softly, wondering if Linda had forgotten to change the sign on the door. It said Open, but there were no other customers inside and it looked to Doris June that the café must still be closed.

"Oh, hi," Linda said as she stepped out from the back kitchen.

Linda had her white chef's apron on over her jeans and there were red tomato spots on it. Her hair seemed to be falling out of some kind of a band at the back of her head and there was a streak of flour on her left cheek.

"I can come back later," Doris June said. "I thought you were open, but I don't really need anything."

"No, come on in," Linda said as she pulled one of the chairs. "I've been wanting to ask your advice anyway."

"Really?" Doris June said as she walked over to the table where Linda was sitting and pulled a chair down for herself.

Linda nodded. "It's about all this fuss over the spaghetti special Aaron wants me to put on the menu."

"Oh, yeah," Doris June said. "That was one of his better ideas, I thought. I remember people used to love your spaghetti sauce. Aaron suggested it because of the

Jazz tie-in, but I think people would love to see it on the menu again anyway."

"I can't remember the sauce," Linda said in defeat. "I've been in the back since I opened and I've been trying to put together the sauce and it doesn't work. The last batch I made tasted like ketchup. Burnt ketchup."

"Well, I remember you used to make that sauce all the time."

Linda nodded and looked at Doris June. "I think I have a mental block. I haven't made it since Duane left, you know?"

"Oh."

"I was hoping you could help me. On account of you got over Curt and never seemed to forget anything important like this."

Linda looked as if she was ready to cry so Doris June patted her pockets to see if she had a tissue. It seemed she was no better at carrying tissues around in her jeans pockets than she had been when she was wearing a suit. She pulled a napkin out of a dispenser on a nearby table though and gave it to Linda.

"Don't worry. I'm sure you haven't really forgotten the recipe," Doris June said. "It's just the stress of this concert and starting to think about Duane again. The recipe will come back to you."

Linda dabbed at her eyes with the napkin. "I'm a chef. How can I forget my grandmother's special recipe?"

Doris June patted the young woman's shoulder. "Maybe you wrote it down somewhere."

Linda shook her head. "I didn't *need* to write it down. I knew it like I knew my own name."

"Well, then, it'll come back to you. Maybe we should just look at your spices and think about how much of each you used." Doris June thought it would be good for Linda to get up and move around. Exercise was always good when one was discouraged.

"How did you ever do it?" Linda looked at Doris June. "When Curt got married to that other woman, you just seemed to take it all in stride. I know I'd cry for a week if

I heard Duane got married, even though I haven't seen him for a good two years."

"I'm sure you'd cope fine if the day came," Doris June said.

"Yeah, I know," Linda said as she folded the napkin and put it in her pocket. "I just hope I do as good as you did. I really admire you for that."

Doris June closed her eyes for a second and then opened them up. "Don't admire me. I was so mad. Furious, actually."

"No," Linda said, surprised.

"Oh, yes," Doris June agreed.

"I didn't know," Linda said softly as she put her hand on Doris June's arm.

"I still don't understand it," Doris June said. "So don't admire me."

Linda smiled. "I admire you even more for being honest with me about it. If I ever do get word that Duane has gotten married, I'm going to call you up and have a good cry with you on the phone."

"You do that."

The two of them sat there for a while.

"Garlic," Linda finally said as she got up. "I'll need to get some fresh garlic. I remember I need to sauté that with some onion. That's the first step. I'll need to go into Miles City for supplies this afternoon if I'm going to make the sauce the right way."

Doris June reached into her pocket and pulled out two twenty-dollar bills. "If you're going to Miles City, could you get some cookies for the concert on Saturday? My mom thinks we need to bake the cookies, but I don't think we'll have time to do that and get the pansy baskets ready for Mother's Day."

"Nobody bakes cookies anymore, especially not for a crowd like that," Linda said as she took the two bills. "What kind do you want?"

"Something with chocolate in them. Teenagers always seem to like chocolate."

"Well, who doesn't?" Linda said, and then gave a whoop. "That's it. Chocolate. I put a little chocolate in the sauce."

"In the spaghetti sauce?"

Linda nodded with a grin. "My grandmother used to call it her secret ingredient.

She didn't use much, but she said it made the tomatoes taste a little more mellow."

Doris June stood up. "Well, I'm glad you've solved the problem."

"Now if I can only remember where Duane kept that old guitar of his. Aaron thought it would make a great decoration to hang on the wall. You know, the guitar that the Jazz Man used to play when he was a nobody."

"You should be proud of him," Doris June said. "I've heard he's become very well-known. As I remember, you were the one who encouraged him to do his first performances here."

Linda nodded. "He always had talent, Duane did."

"Maybe, someday…" Doris June began.

Linda shook her head. "He invited me out to visit him a while back and I went. He lives in a whole different world now. I couldn't live in that world even if it meant being by Duane. Which it wouldn't really—he had so many other people around him."

Doris June nodded. "I guess people change."

"Although, it would be nice to have a wall of the café to remember him by," Linda said. "It'd be nice to hear his name once in a while. Not a day goes by that I don't wonder where he is and if he's okay. I mean with drugs and everything, I wonder if he's all right. At least you always knew where Curt was."

Doris June nodded. She'd never considered that a blessing before, but maybe it was. She had always known Curt was safe and well. If he'd been seriously sick, she would have heard about it.

Doris June helped Linda put the chairs down before she walked back to her mother's house.

"Time to go," Doris June said as they put their jackets on to drive out to the farm. "There's no need to do everything yourself. I know you're not used to asking for help, but it's time for you to do it when you need it."

"Well, I don't always need help." Mrs.

Hargrove bristled. "It's just all that's going on this weekend."

"I didn't mean you always need help," Doris June said as she opened the car door for her mother. "I mean there's no shame in asking for help when you do need it."

"Well, of course not."

"What I really mean," Doris June said as she held the door open while her mother arranged herself inside the car, "is that I would like to give you more help these days."

"Well, that's different," her mother said with a pleased look on her face.

Doris June walked around to the driver's side of the car and slid inside. "What would you think if I came home more often? Maybe every couple of months or so?"

"Why, that would be wonderful."

"Yeah, it would be," Doris June said as she started the car.

It was time she came home, Doris June told herself. Even if it was only for scattered weekends every few months, it would be enough time for her to be more a part of her mother's life and more a part of the life of Dry Creek, too. She'd be able to do things she hadn't been able to do in her annual visits. It would give her a chance to see if she should make a permanent move to Dry Creek, too. She shouldn't let the past bind her as it had. If it hadn't been for her pride, she might have already moved back to Dry Creek. She surely would have researched doing it at least. She didn't like the fact that she'd let the past determine her future. This whole concert thing might be just what she needed to let the past go. She surely hoped so.

CHAPTER ELEVEN

CURT HAD SPENT the morning carefully digging pansies out of the ground and putting them in his wheelbarrow. He wanted to have things ready to go when Doris June and Mrs. Hargrove got here. It was late Friday morning and he hoped, with the moss, that the pansies would be okay in their baskets until Sunday if they were kept cool and watered.

He hadn't realized until this year that Mrs. Hargrove had chosen such a delicate flower for her Mother's Day presentations all those years ago. As he thought about it he wondered why she hadn't chosen a geranium or a mum. Those were two flowers that were strong enough to endure almost any kind of neglect. Then again, maybe she didn't want these floral gifts for the town's mothers to be too hearty. Maybe there was something about appreciating motherhood that required someone to pay attention.

The whole motherhood thing was a mystery to Curt. He knew, without being told, that Ben suffered from not having had a mother in his life, but Curt had never known what to do about it. Ben's mother was nowhere to be found, and even if Curt did manage to find her, he knew she wouldn't come back and be Ben's mother. His ex-wife had never been fond of relationships where she wasn't the center of attention and a child wasn't just a reflector of happy thoughts.

Curt had wondered often over the years how he could have been so foolish when he'd married. He knew part of it was his impatience as a young man. He wanted quick results with everyone—his parents and Doris June. He had not understood that a good life might require some waiting and that, just because Doris June wasn't really ready to run away with him, it didn't mean she didn't love him.

The irony was that patience was the one big lesson he had learned since then.

He still had to watch himself to be sure, but, usually, Curt found he could slow his steps now and wait for things to develop. He wondered sometimes if his attention to his own lessons had resulted in Ben being too timid. It was as if his son had become the opposite of what Curt was like at his age.

That's one of the reasons Curt was glad Ben was working on this concert. It would do his son good to get up and perform for people. Ben was due some applause in life and the teenagers around Dry Creek were good kids and would see he got it.

If doing the concert meant that Curt had to get up in front of the kids of Dry Creek and admit his mistakes, then so be it. Curt wasn't proud of the mistakes he had made in his life, but he was willing to talk about them with others if it could save some other young hothead from doing the things he had done.

Curt had even looked in the hall closet this morning and found his old letterman jacket. There was the figure of a cowboy on the back for the Miles City basketball team.

Throughout high school either he or Doris June wore that jacket. They passed it back and forth so it carried both of their scents. He'd left it in his room at home when he joined the army and his father had kept it for him until he came home. Curt figured Doris June would enjoy seeing the jacket, so he'd bring it to the concert.

Curt heard Mrs. Hargrove's car coming even though he had his back to the road.

"Good morning," Mrs. Hargrove called as he turned around. She waved to him from the car window.

Curt walked over to the car. "Why don't you let me look at your car for a minute? I can hear there's something wrong."

"We can fix it later," Mrs. Hargrove said as she opened her car door. "First, we need to get the baskets going."

"Yes, ma'am," Curt said as he watched Doris June get out of the other side of the car.

"Where's Charley?" Mrs. Hargrove asked as she walked toward Curt.

"He'll be here soon," Curt said. "He

wanted to make another batch of cookies. The first batch burned."

"I didn't think Charley knew how to make cookies," Mrs. Hargrove said.

"Neither did I, but he's doing it."

"See." Mrs. Hargrove turned to Doris June. "Even Charley knows that the cookies have to be homemade."

"Mom doesn't think we should buy cookies for the concert," Doris June explained to Curt as she walked over to where he had the pansies in the wheelbarrow.

"Almost everything the kids eat anymore comes wrapped in plastic," Curt said as he followed Doris June over to the wheelbarrow and then turned his head to say something to Mrs. Hargrove. "Don't worry about the kids. They'll appreciate anything."

Mrs. Hargrove grunted. "Nobody bought cookies in my day."

Curt grinned. "I'm sure they didn't. That's why my dad is back home mixing up his oatmeal cookies."

"Well, we just want the concert to go well," Mrs. Hargrove said as she picked up a shovel.

"The concert will be fine," Curt said as he reached over and put his hand on the shovel. "There's plenty to do with the baskets, you don't need to lift a shovel."

"That's right, Mother," Doris June agreed when she turned around from the pansies she was digging up. "There's enough to do with those ribbons inside. Remember, we're cutting thirty-inch lengths of ribbon to make bows?"

"And we still need someone to put the baskets in stacks of twelve," Curt said. "That's about how many baskets we can fill with the pansies in a wheelbarrow."

"Fine, I'll go inside and sit down." Mrs. Hargrove put her hands up in a sign of surrender. "I was just trying to be helpful."

"You're more than helpful, Mother." Doris June stood up straight and looked directly at her mother. "You're the reason we're here."

Mrs. Hargrove brightened. "That's right."

"In some ways, you've already done your part," Doris June said. "So relax if you want."

Mrs. Hargrove nodded as she started to walk toward the old farmhouse. "I just might do that."

Doris June watched her mother until she entered the house and then she looked over at Curt. "Give her two minutes and she'll be scrubbing the windows in there."

Curt nodded. "It's hard to change your nature."

Doris June nodded and then turned to push her shovel into the dirt again.

Curt knew this was a natural opening to talk to Doris June about the impatience that had driven him as a young man and how it had done so much to damage his life. She hadn't been here very long this morning, though, and he thought he should wait and let them work shoulder to shoulder for a bit. He didn't want to rush into any serious discussion unless he was sure the timing was right. He'd already made his mistakes with rushing Doris June and he wanted to be sure she was open to listening to him before he confessed his failings.

"Are you having a good time with your mother?" Curt asked after a couple of minutes of silence. "I can tell she's happy you're home."

Doris June nodded. "I think she misses me more now that she's getting older."

"Yeah, things change."

Together they finished filling the wheelbarrow with pansies, all in their own clump of roots and dirt.

"I bet your dad's glad that you're back," Doris June said as she straightened up.

"Yeah, he is." Curt tilted the wheelbarrow up and started to push it to the house. He looked over to be sure Doris June was coming with him. "My dad didn't want to sell the farm and I don't know what he would have done if I hadn't wanted to come back and take over. Besides, Ben and I were both tired of Chicago and I didn't want to keep raising Ben there."

Doris June nodded as she put out a hand to steady the wheelbarrow. "I know my mom is glad that you're back and want to rent the land on our farm. She's not ready to sell the place, either."

"Well, maybe you'll want the farm someday," Curt said.

Doris June just grunted.

By that time, they were on the porch of the farmhouse and they were ready to start putting the pansies into baskets. Curt figured he had done what he could to plant the thought in Doris June's head. He'd have to wait and see if she took hold of it with any interest.

They had several baskets put together when Curt heard another vehicle drive up to the house.

"It's Charley," Mrs. Hargrove announced as she walked over to the door and opened it. "What took you so long?"

Mrs. Hargrove walked out on the porch to greet his father.

Curt could see out the window as his father held up a brown paper bag.

"I take back everything I said about store-bought cookies being okay," Curt said as he winked at Doris June. She had just turned around to look at him. Curt pointed to where his father was walking toward the door. "I think we hit the jackpot."

"Cookies," Mrs. Hargrove announced as she led Charley into the kitchen.

"Oatmeal raisin," Charley added. "The pick of the batch."

"I thought you'd save the best for the kids," Curt said.

Charley shook his head. "The workers need to eat."

"I'll go along with that," Doris June said as she held up her hands. "Just let me wash up a bit."

Doris June stood at the kitchen sink and let the water run over her hands. She'd used a bar of soap that sat beside the sink. She didn't know what Curt was thinking about when he mentioned that she might want the farm someday. She wondered if he was repeating words he'd heard her mother say.

It hadn't escaped Doris June's notice that her mother had kept everything about the house here livable. She still kept the electrical running and had the drapes all sealed away in plastic tubs in the corner of the living room. The wooden furniture had been left standing in its place. The books had been moved and all of the furniture, like the sofa and living room chairs, had been given away to neighbors long ago. But it wouldn't take much to make the house usable again. Even if she never farmed the land, she would probably want to spend summers at the house like her family used to if she moved back to Dry Creek.

It unnerved her though that Curt had mentioned the idea. The Curt she remembered never just mentioned anything. He had a definite opinion on everything. The fact that he hadn't urged her to move back and open the house hadn't escaped her notice. He'd asked the question very neutrally. That wasn't like him. She wondered if it meant he was just seeking information and didn't have an opinion.

She shook her head. She didn't see how she could move back to the farm. She'd see him driving his tractor around the land every spring and see him harvesting every fall.

"Save some cookies for Doris June," Charley said.

Doris June finished drying her hands.

"I was saving some," Curt protested. He was holding the bag. "See, these are her three right here."

"Well, okay, then," Charley said.

"The kids are going to love these," Mrs. Hargrove said as she held up one of the cookies. "I don't think I've tasted a better oatmeal cookie, and here all these years you've been coming to me to get cookies."

"Well, I didn't say I like to bake them. I'd rather brand a hundred calves than stir up a dozen cookies. I can hardly read the recipe anymore. And all of those teaspoons and tablespoons. I don't know why they don't just use a cup for everything."

Mrs. Hargrove looked at her cookie more closely. "You did measure things, didn't you?"

Charley nodded. "I didn't want to, though. It about drove me crazy. And waiting to take them out of the oven. I think there should be a better way."

Curt smiled as he handed over the rest of the cookies to Doris June.

Mrs. Hargrove and Charley walked out onto the porch.

"You can see where I got my impatient nature," Curt said to Doris June softly. "It's a wonder I waited until you were seventeen to ask you to elope with me. I thought of it when I first got my license. You were so beautiful."

"You just want a share of my cookies," Doris June said as she looked into the brown bag. She hoped her cheeks weren't pink. She wasn't sure how to take Curt's teasing.

Curt chuckled. "Well, I wouldn't say no to another one if you insist. I had no idea my dad could bake."

Doris June handed him one of her cookies. "Well, what did you think he did for meals before you moved home? He'd been on his own for years by then."

Curt nodded. "I never thought of that. He said he didn't cook and I just started doing it. I thought maybe he ate with your mother or something."

"Every meal?" Doris June said. "And they didn't have the café back then, either."

"I bet he can even make pot roast," Curt said. "I came home early from plowing one day and he was pulling a pot roast out of the oven. I thought your mother had brought it over."

"Well, our parents can surprise us," Doris June said as she took the last cookie from the bag. "At least, they don't seem romantically inclined anymore."

"Yeah, I noticed," Curt said. "I kind of miss it."

"You *miss* it?" Doris June took a bite of the cookie.

Curt shrugged. "Yeah, I kind of thought maybe they'd go for it. I mean, they've been friends forever."

"Just because they're friends, doesn't mean they have any business getting married. Getting married is very complicated."

"Is it?" Curt asked.

Doris June nodded. "It's a business contract, for starters. There's money involved and houses and things."

"I don't think our parents would let those kinds of things stop them from getting married," Curt said. "And, if they were worried about it, they could draw up a prenuptial agreement."

"Oh, I can't see them doing something like that."

"Well, no, I can't, either," Curt said.

"But, if they were worried about it, they'd have sense enough to do something like that rather than just not get married."

"Maybe."

"I know I would sign a prenuptial," Curt said. "If the woman I was marrying had, say, a huge retirement account or a house or something. I wouldn't let money stand in the way of getting married. Not after all this time."

"Well, no one said it should stand in the way," Doris June said. "I'm just saying it's a complication."

Neither Curt nor Doris June was aware that their voices were rising until Mrs. Hargrove stuck her head back in the kitchen. "Everything okay in here?"

"Oh, yeah," Doris June said. "We were just talking."

"Some hot topic," Charley said as he joined Mrs. Hargrove in the doorway.

"I think we need to go get another batch of pansies," Curt said as he started walking toward the door. "The day will be gone before we know it."

Doris June walked with Curt to the door.

When they were on the porch, Curt picked up the wheelbarrow and started to push it back to the pansy patch.

Mrs. Hargrove watched her daughter and Curt make their way past both cars and down the road a little way to the flowers.

"They think we're deaf," Mrs. Hargrove said.

Charley grunted. "I don't mind them arguing, but I don't want them arguing over us."

"I'm not sure it was about us," Mrs. Hargrove said. "Still, I don't want them to get mad at each other before they have a chance to have a few good times together."

"I don't know," Charley said. "Those two always did do things their own way."

"Unless we stepped in, of course," Mrs. Hargrove said.

"Now, Edith," Charley said. "I thought we agreed that we did the best we could back then. There's no point in you continuing to feel guilty."

"I know. It just comes on me here and there," Mrs. Hargrove said. She didn't think Charley even realized he'd called her by her first name. She hoped he would do it more often. She kind of liked it.

"Well, I guess if you feel guilty, you'll at least have something to say at this concert when they want the people behind the stop sign to talk," Charley said.

"Oh, but that's not us," Mrs. Hargrove said in alarm. "That's just Doris June and Curt."

"I don't think that's what the state guy said."

"Oh, but surely, he couldn't have meant us. I wouldn't know what to say."

"Well, me neither," Charley said. "That's why I baked some cookies. So I could say I've already done my part."

"Oh, dear me," Mrs. Hargrove said. "Maybe I should go home and bake cookies, too. I could make sugar cookies."

"I always did like your sugar cookies," Charley said.

"You're not getting any. Not now that you can bake your own."

It took a few more hours to finish up enough pansy baskets that everyone agreed it was time to quit for the day. Ben and

Lucy would be home from school and Doris June finally admitted that her back was beginning to hurt from bending over to pick up the pansies.

"Well, you should have told me earlier that your back was feeling it," Mrs. Hargrove said. "I could have switched places with you for a while. There's nothing to this ribbon business."

Actually, Mrs. Hargrove had thought about going out and switching places with Doris June a couple of times, but then she'd heard bursts of laughter from the pansy patch and decided to wait.

"We don't need you to be bending like this," Doris June said to her mother from the doorway. "I'm glad you had me come down to help."

"You're always a big help." Mrs. Hargrove set down the scissors she was using to cut the ribbon and walked to where Doris June was standing.

"We got most of the work done," Curt said as he stepped onto the porch. "A little more tomorrow and we'll be set."

Doris June nodded and stretched her back.

"Give us a call when you know what time we should come over tomorrow," Mrs. Hargrove said as she and Doris June started to walk toward their car.

Mrs. Hargrove had seen the look in Curt's eyes as he watched Doris June stretch and she finally knew that she and Charley had done the right thing by getting their kids together again. It wasn't passion exactly that she'd seen in Curt's eyes. It was more of a look of contentment. Curt was glad to have Doris June back. Of course, Mrs. Hargrove didn't know how her daughter felt about being back. That could be a problem.

CHAPTER TWELVE

DORIS JUNE ALMOST felt like putting on her navy suit when she woke up Saturday morning. It was only six-thirty and she already felt the day was going to get away from her. Of course, even in her suit, she wouldn't be in charge of the day, so she decided to stick with her jeans. She did iron a white blouse to wear simply because the day was going to end with a concert, and a white blouse would be dressy enough for that.

Besides, white implied neutrality and she was trying to keep her emotions in that gear. She'd gotten a little off track talking with Curt yesterday, because he'd sounded so friendly. A time or two, she almost thought he was flirting with her. She couldn't afford to mistake his friendliness for anything more than what it was,

though, so she was going to do everything
she could to keep things in the neutral zone.

Her mother was still sleeping, so Doris
June decided to walk over to the café after
she got dressed. She figured Lucy would be
there early. The teenager probably wouldn't
be waiting tables, but Lucy would have
gotten a ride into Dry Creek when Linda
came to work and she'd be using the café
to organize the concert. It made sense. It's
what Doris June would do in Lucy's place.
Ben would probably be there, too.

Doris June figured she had guessed right
when she found Charley's car parked near
the café. She could hear the soft sounds
of someone strumming on a guitar from
inside the café. That had to be Ben practicing.

It had rained some during the night and
the ground was damp.

The smell of coffee greeted Doris June
when she set foot on the café porch. She
scraped off her shoes and twisted the door-
knob. The door opened easily and Doris
June had a good view. It looked like everyone inside had already been awake for

hours. At least they were already doing something productive.

Linda was walking around talking into a handheld phone. Lucy was marking out big black letters on a piece of white cardboard. It looked like she was making a No Smoking sign. Ben was sitting at a table in the corner, frowning to himself and playing a guitar.

"But you've got to stop him," Linda was saying into the phone as she gestured for Doris June to have a seat. "You had no right to ask him for that anyway."

"I hope nothing's wrong." Doris June took a seat at the table where Lucy was working. "Linda doesn't sound too happy."

Lucy looked up from her cardboard. "She thinks Aaron has gone too far with all this publicity."

Doris June could still hear Linda complaining to someone on the phone.

"I don't see how he could have gone too far," Doris June said, and she kept her voice loud enough so Linda could hear it if she chose. Maybe it would help Linda to hear another perspective. "He's only had a day to get the word out. He probably had to move fast to get the schools in Billings lined up with what's happening."

"He went for the news media," Lucy said as she turned her cardboard sideways.

"Well, I can't imagine they're very interested," Doris June said, as much to comfort herself as to calm down Linda. "Just because Aaron sent out a press release, it doesn't mean any paper will pay any attention to it. The concert will be over before they can send someone out to cover it anyway."

Linda pressed the disconnect button on the phone.

"He's asked for an endorsement from Duane," Linda said as she stepped over to the table and sat down in a chair next to Doris June. She set the phone on the table in front of her.

"Your Duane? The Jazz Man?" Doris June asked in surprise. "How would he expect to get an endorsement from him? As big as he is in the music world, the Jazz Man must have a publicist who screens those requests. He doesn't even know Aaron."

"No, but he knows me." Linda bit off her words in disgust. "And Aaron used my name. He didn't even say it was him asking for the endorsement. So now Duane is going to think I'm trying to make money off him." Linda looked around until she saw where Ben was playing guitar. "I already brought his old guitar into the café. Ben even found some old picks of Duane's. We're going to have a regular Graceland happening here if we're not careful. Wouldn't Duane get a laugh out of that?"

"Well, I don't think he'd know exactly." Doris June offered what comfort she could. "Even if Aaron got through to Duane's publicist, the concert is tonight. The publicist probably just collects these requests for endorsements and gives them to Duane once a month or so."

"Once a year would be better," Linda muttered, and shook her head. "I can't believe Aaron did that. I haven't asked Duane for anything since he left. Not even his share of the rent for that month when he split, which technically he owed me since he didn't give me notice or anything."

Doris June knew how the technicalities of a breakup could eat away at a person. She heard the sound of boots on the porch of the café. "I wouldn't worry about Aaron. I don't think he would have got too far with Duane."

The door to the café opened, but Doris June didn't turn around to see who it was. She didn't want Linda to think she wasn't getting her undivided attention. Besides, Doris June already knew it had to be Charley or Curt entering the café; Ben couldn't have driven into town by himself.

Doris June patted Linda's arm. "It'll be okay. You'll see."

"You'd be surprised what Aaron can do," Linda said, and then hesitated. "He's used your name, too."

"Me? I don't even know Duane. Or anybody famous, for that matter."

CURT STOOD BY the café door and watched the pink rise in Doris June's face. He could hear her words plainly. She might not be famous, but she was sure pretty. He'd thought about her all last night. He was trying not to get ahead of himself, but Curt thought things were going rather well between Doris June and him. They'd almost talked together like friends yesterday while they dug up pansies. He was beginning to hope they could work their way to becoming more than friends in time.

Curt took a step farther into the café, but he didn't want to interrupt the women. Linda was already leaning closer to Doris June, as though she didn't want to say her words too loud.

"Aaron thinks you're famous," Linda finally said to Doris June. "Because you work for a television station."

"But I'm not even on the air," Doris June answered in amazement. "Nobody's famous in the sales department."

Linda shrugged. "All I know is that he called the station and got some weatherman there to promise to pass a picture of the concert on to the news team. He e-mailed the guy a press release to go with it. Aaron said the weatherman, a Mr. Jackson, spoke very highly of you."

"He's going to give them a picture of Lucy and Ben singing?" Doris June clarified. "That's okay. I'm sure the news team will say thanks, but no thanks, but he's welcome to try. Anybody can try."

Linda shook her head. "You don't understand. The only Anchorage angle is you. He's going to give the weatherman a press release of you talking about eloping."

Curt wasn't prepared for the look of absolute horror that came over Doris June's face.

"He can't do that," Doris June said. "I have to work with those people."

There was silence for a moment.

"I think he already did it," Linda finally said softly. "He threw together a news release from what he learned yesterday."

Doris June just sat there. Curt noticed that her face wasn't pink anymore. It was as white as her blouse.

"It's not so bad," Curt finally said as he walked closer to her and pulled up a chair.

"Everybody does crazy things when they're teenagers."

"I don't," Doris June said, and then caught herself. "Well, I did, I guess, but it wasn't like me."

Curt had to admit he might have misread how much progress he'd made in his relationship with Doris June. He had thought she was starting to feel friendly toward him again, but she looked so appalled that she'd almost eloped with him twenty-five years ago that he was no longer sure how she felt. In fact, when he thought about it, he didn't know if he should be insulted that she looked so horrified.

"Maybe we can get it back," Curt finally offered. He couldn't waste his energy on worrying about insults. "I could call this weatherman and explain what happened—"

Doris June looked even more stricken.

"Or not," Curt continued. "I'll do whatever you want."

Doris June swallowed. "No, I can call and talk to Randy."

Curt frowned. Now that the weatherman had a name that didn't start with Mr., he liked him even less. He must be a Randall or Randolph, so why didn't the man just use his name? Randy sounded a little too cozy.

"Do you have his phone number?"

"I can reach him at the station."

"I don't suppose he's married?" Curt asked, just to be sure he wasn't getting bothered by something he shouldn't be.

Doris June shook her head as she stood up. "I don't know what I panicked for. I just need to go back to Mom's place and call the station. Randy owes me a favor anyway. He'll keep the news release to himself."

Curt supposed that was good news. Part of him was glad that this Randy would read the news release at least. Somebody needed to tell that guy that Doris June wasn't exactly available.

"You're sure you don't want me to talk to him?" Curt offered again. "I can tell him it was all my idea."

"Well, he'll know that's not true," Doris June snapped as she headed toward the door. "It takes two fools to elope."

Curt watched Doris June leave and let the door slam behind her.

Only then did Linda put her hand on his arm. "It's not always foolish, you know. Eloping is sometimes the right thing, even if it's at the wrong time."

Curt looked over at her and grimaced. "My timing never has been very good."

"You and me both," Linda said as she stood up. "Care for some coffee? On the house? I have a feeling we're both going to need it today."

Curt nodded. He knew he wasn't going to get any plowing done this morning. If he wasn't going to be working on pansy baskets, he'd be hauling his old pickup into town for the concert tonight.

IT DIDN'T TAKE long for Doris June to reach Randy on the telephone. She sat at her mother's dining table and scolded him for even agreeing to Aaron's plan. Randy assured her he would throw away the copy he'd printed of the news release and delete the file from the e-mail Aaron had sent.

"The guy's a pitbull when it comes to

getting what he wants," Randy said. "You might want to ask him if he wants to work in the sales department up here."

"It doesn't do any good to make a sale if it's unsold the minute the salesman walks away," Doris June said. "That's why we build relationships with our clients."

"Yeah, well, the guy should be doing something."

"I think he'll do enough damage right where he is," Doris June said. "And, thanks. I'll buy you lunch when I get back."

"It's a date," Randy said cheerfully.

Doris June nodded. It was the closest thing to a date she had to look forward to in the near future.

Doris June was feeling better by the time she returned to the café. She decided Linda must be feeling better, too, because she heard someone singing in the kitchen.

"She's making the sauce," Lucy said as she looked up from the new sign she was making. "I think she's got it right for a change."

"Well, things are looking up for everyone," Doris June said as she sat down in one of the chairs. She'd wait for Linda to come out of the kitchen before she announced that she'd stopped the news release about her.

Doris June knew, of course, that the release never would have made it onto the news broadcast; but she didn't want it to be handed around to the people in the station. She valued her privacy, and when she'd heard what Aaron had done, for a minute she had thought she'd have to endure again all the pity of twenty-five years ago.

When she thought about it, Doris June realized it would, of course, never be like it was twenty-five years ago. For one thing, the people in Anchorage weren't as interested in her love life as the people in Dry Creek had always been. That probably had to do with the fact that her mother lived here, Doris June decided.

Linda came out of the kitchen and raised her spoon in the air. "I did it! Grandma's recipe is back!"

"Now, write it down," Doris June advised. "Right now, while you know it."

Linda grinned. "Sometimes, you can undo the bad that's happened."

Doris June couldn't deny the truth of what Linda had said.

"You'll see," Linda said as she turned to go back into the kitchen. "Mark my words. You'll see."

CHAPTER THIRTEEN

"So, do you think you'll ever forgive me?" Curt asked. He leaned back on his shovel and looked at Doris June. He couldn't figure her out. One minute she seemed fine with their past and the next she was going all prickly on him. He thought spending some time alone with her in the pansy patch would give him a better understanding of where she was at, but it hadn't and he was running out of time.

It was late afternoon, and Curt figured this might be their last chance to be alone to talk this through. Both of their parents were so afraid of what questions might come up at the concert tonight that they'd stayed at Mrs. Hargrove's place to bake cookies, leaving Curt and Doris June to do what they could to finish the pansy baskets. Curt knew he couldn't count on their parents leaving them alone once the concert was over.

"It all happened a long time ago," Doris June slowly said as she used her shovel to lift a clump of dirt with a pansy sticking out of it and place it in the wheelbarrow. "I'd be foolish to still hold a grudge. Grudges only hurt the people who hold them."

Curt noticed she wasn't looking him in the eye. Instead, she seemed very concerned with the pansy.

"That doesn't exactly answer my question." Curt touched Doris June's arm to get her attention. He wanted to see the expression in her eyes. "I know it was hard for you."

"How would you know that? You hit the stop sign and then you took off and left me sitting in the sheriff's office," Doris June answered him calmly. She did finally look at him, though, and Curt shivered. She was mad at him, all right. She looked at him as politely as she would if he were a new specimen of the insect family.

"Here, let me take that." Curt held out

his hand for Doris June's shovel. She had started punching it into the dirt at her feet and he didn't think she even realized it. He was afraid she'd accidentally hit one of her feet with it. Or, maybe hit one of his feet, not so accidentally.

Doris June gave up her shovel without complaint and brushed her hair back from the side of her face. She did not seem to realize she had a little bit of dirt on her hand and was leaving a streak of prime farmland on her cheek while she did it. Curt resisted the urge to rub the dirt off or to get sidetracked by telling her about it. The dirt made her look kind of cute anyway. Fortunately, she'd exchanged her white blouse for the old sweatshirt before they drove out to the farm.

"I left the sheriff's office that evening because I remembered the lights were still on in the pickup," Curt said. "I didn't want the battery to run down."

Curt remembered that night. How could he forget it? It had just become dark and the air was cool. Inside the cab of his pickup, however, things were warm and cozy. He had been a proud bridegroom heading off to get married, with Doris June snuggled close under his arm. He was claiming his future, his bride. And then in a minute, it all changed. Instead of being a bridegroom, he was being scolded as if he was a little kid. He was embarrassed in front of Doris June. "I didn't think you much wanted me around, anyway."

At this Doris June's eyes blazed. "It would have been nice for you to stick around and answer the questions."

"I thought we'd already been over all of the possible questions." Curt figured it was good for Doris June to get angry with him and he was going to keep her going until she said it all. Maybe when she got it out of her system, she'd let it go. He pressed on. "I'd already told the sheriff what had happened. How many details did he need? It was almost dark and we hit the stop sign. I wasn't speeding. No one cut in front of us. I wasn't blinded by the sun. I was driving and should have been more careful. I hit the sign. That was pretty much it. Nobody was even hurt."

"They could have been." Doris June pressed her lips together.

"I asked you if you were all right. Whether you had whiplash, or anything."

Doris June glared at him. "How would I have known if I had something wrong? I'd never been in a car accident before. I didn't know what to expect."

He hadn't known she'd been scared. Maybe if he'd known, he'd have hugged her instead of running away to hide.

"I didn't mean for it to happen," Curt said softly. He made sure Doris June was looking at his eyes. He wanted her to know he was sincere. "I was stupid to get mad and walk off like that, but I never meant for any of it to happen. The sheriff was only doing his job. I was just a hothead back then."

Doris June was still looking at him, but she blinked.

Curt decided he should keep on with it. "I've changed since then, though. I'd like to prove it to you. Isn't there something I can do to make it right between us? I'm so sorry."

"You broke my heart," Doris June said as she reached out and picked up her shovel again. "I learned my lesson with you that night."

Curt forced himself to take another breath. "And what lesson might that be?"

Doris June ignored his question. "I think the wheelbarrow is about full. I can work on the baskets inside the house now."

And, with that, she walked away and took the wheelbarrow with her.

Curt decided that Doris June had, indeed, learned a lesson from him that night twenty-five years ago. She'd walked away when things were getting interesting, just like he had back then. The only difference was that she didn't look as if she regretted it one little bit and he would do anything for the chance to make changes to that night.

DORIS JUNE COULDN'T wait to park the wheelbarrow on the porch and slam the door behind her as she stomped into the house. The sound of the door shutting should let Curt know their conversation was ended. She didn't understand why Curt couldn't just let things be between them. She had actually started to enjoy being around him. And then he had to bring up the elopement. You would think they had been planning to commit high treason the way everybody seemed to want to keep talking about that particular day from the past.

Well, Doris June thought as she picked up a basket, she was going to forget there even was such a thing as an elopement. She slammed the basket down on the kitchen table and yanked a precut section of yellow ribbon off the spool where her mother had rewound it. No one could say it had been her idea to elope anyway. She poked at the ribbon until it became a bow and then she pushed a couple of pansies into the basket. If she got a chance to talk to the kids at the concert tonight, she was going to be sure and warn every one of them to never, ever elope.

Doris June looked at the basket she had just made. Something about it didn't look right. She frowned. Her mother had made those bows look so easy. Maybe there would be time to put the bows on the baskets tonight after the concert. Ben and Lucy had volunteered to help with the baskets when the concert was over. Lucy would be good with bows. One way or the other, every Mother's Day basket would have a perfectly formed bow on its handle on Sunday morning.

Curt kept his eye on the house while he finished digging up the rest of the pansies. He decided to put the clumps of dirt he'd just dug up in the plastic containers Doris June had left on the hillside. He didn't want to rush her by going down to get the wheelbarrow so he could move the pansies, but he couldn't wait forever. He looked up at the sun. It was about four o'clock and he still had to do some chores at his own farm before he went in to the concert, unless, of course, his father remembered to go out to the farm and do them.

AT THAT SAME time, back in Dry Creek, Charley looked at the clock in Mrs. Hargrove's kitchen and thought about evening chores. Nelson men had been thinking about their chores at that same time for over a hundred years.

"I wonder if that son of mine will remember the chickens," Charley muttered as he carefully used a spatula to slide a row of chocolate-chip cookies from the baking tray to the cooling rack. "And the horses will want more hay."

"Maybe he has other things on his mind besides chores," Mrs. Hargrove said a little smugly. "We left them alone together, you know."

Charley grunted. "One of them's probably dead by now."

"Oh, you." Mrs. Hargrove waved a cookie spoon in the air. She was making another batch of dough. "I don't think things are going so badly. They're talking at least."

Charley shrugged as he scooped the last cookie off the tray and flipped it into his hand. "Well, we've done all we can, that's for sure."

Charley took a bite out of the warm cookie.

"Do you remember that night? We stood in this very living room with my wife and your husband. Doris June was up in her room crying and we didn't even know where Curt was then. You suggested that maybe together we could figure out what to do about everything."

Mrs. Hargrove nodded. "I remember."

"Well, what happened?"

There was silence for a minute.

"I think *I* happened," Mrs. Hargrove confessed in a rush. "That's why I've felt so bad about this whole thing. I knew what I wanted to do and that was lock Doris June up until she turned thirty."

Charley nodded. "Well, she's turned thirty, now what?"

"She tells me she still dates," Mrs. Hargrove said a little sadly. "But I don't think she does. I mean not really. Her heart's not in it."

"Well, maybe she doesn't want to get married. Not everyone does."

Mrs. Hargrove looked up at Charley. "She wanted to get married back then. A woman doesn't change that much between seventeen and forty."

"Of course they do," Charley said. "They change in all kinds of ways."

"How do you know that?"

"I read magazines. I keep informed about what the younger generation thinks."

"I thought maybe Curt had said something to you about Doris June. I thought maybe they'd talked about whether either one of them wants to get married. I mean, just in general."

Charley grunted. "No, he hasn't said a thing about what they've talked about. I've been meaning to ask him, but—"

Mrs. Hargrove nodded. "We've already butted into their business enough."

"This time I think we really do need to leave it up to them to sort out," Charley said softly.

Mrs. Hargrove sighed and took one of the warm cookies, too. "Yes, I think you're right." She sighed again. "It's just—"

Charley nodded. "It's hard to accept, I know, but they might not want to get married again after all of these years."

Mrs. Hargrove nodded as she put her cookie on a scrap of napkin so she could turn around and pull the next pan of cookies from the oven. "I know Doris June likes her independence. She's a great organizer and she's a wonder when she's in charge. Boom. Boom. Things get done."

"She takes after her mother," Charley said as he took a sudden interest in his shoe. He felt a little cowardly asking the question when Edith had her back to him and was bent over pulling the cookie sheet out of the oven. "Makes me wonder if you've ever thought about getting married again."

"Me?" Mrs. Hargrove stood up so fast she dropped the cookie pan on the floor. "Oh, dear. Look what I've done."

"You didn't hurt yourself, did you? Those burns can be nasty." Charley grabbed a towel from the counter so he could help pick up the pan.

"Fortunately, the pan landed right-side up," Mrs. Hargrove said. "The cookies are all okay."

"That's good," Charley said as he helped

Mrs. Hargrove lift the pan of cookies to the counter. She had hold of one end of it with a pot holder and he had hold of the other end with the towel. Charley decided he should wait to ask any other sensitive questions until there was nothing hot flying around to burn one of them.

"We'll keep those cookies to the side," Mrs. Hargrove said as she frowned at the cookies on the pan. "They didn't fall on the floor or anything, but we can't be too careful."

Charley nodded. "We can never be too careful."

It was odd, Charley decided. It didn't matter what age they were—the Nelson men always had a tendency to shy away from pressing for a commitment when there was the least sign of trouble. He wondered if it was in their genes. He could only hope that Ben would have better sense, but the boy was the shyest of them all.

Mrs. Hargrove had the next batch of cookies baked when Charley heard Curt's pickup pull up outside.

"That'll be Doris June," Charley said. "And Curt bringing her back."

Mrs. Hargrove nodded. "She'll want to change for the concert."

Charley brightened. "I don't suppose you two are going to wear those pretty dresses again?"

"We'd freeze to death," Mrs. Hargrove said. "Those things don't have a shred of warmth to them."

"Yeah, I suppose not."

"That's one reason my ginghams are so good. They keep a person's bones warm at least."

"Nothing wrong with your ginghams," Charley said as he stood up. "I should go help Curt with the chores. Ben is still over at the café practicing away and I can guarantee he hasn't given any thought to the chores."

Mrs. Hargrove looked up from her cookies. "If you think of it, talk to Curt about—you know."

Charley nodded as he turned to walk to the door. He could always ask his son for advice. Curt would get a chuckle out of that. Maybe the two of them could form a support group for men wondering what to do about their feelings for the Hargrove women. Support groups were real popular these days. He'd read about them in those magazines he'd gotten from Linda.

Doris June smiled at Charley as she passed him coming out of her mother's house at the same time as she was going in. He smiled back at her.

"Doris June had dirt on her cheek," Charley announced as he opened the passenger door on Curt's pickup and climbed inside.

"Pansies are messy business," Curt said as he shifted into Reverse.

"Oh, I thought maybe she got it from being kissed."

Curt turned to glare at his father. "She didn't get it from being kissed by me, if that's what you're asking." Curt paused. "You can pass the word along to Mrs. Hargrove if you want. I'm sure she's curious, too, how your plans are going."

Charley mumbled something that could

mean anything. "So, what are you wearing to the concert tonight?"

MEANWHILE, DORIS JUNE was being asked that same question by her mother. Not the kissing one. The wardrobe one.

"I was going to wear that white blouse and the blue pants that go with my suit," Doris June said. She'd already eaten one of the cookies her mother had given her. "But I'm thinking maybe I should give Aaron a break and wear something from high school. After all, the concert's for the kids."

"You still like kids, don't you?" Mrs. Hargrove asked. She stared at her pot holder so she'd look subtle. "I mean, even if you don't want to get married and have any of your own."

"I've always liked kids," Doris June said as she looked at her mother. "You know that. Why wouldn't I like kids?"

Mrs. Hargrove shrugged. "Well, they would limit your independence. I know how you like your independence."

"Well, yes, but if I had kids, I'd make

adjustments," Doris June said as she kept looking at her mother. "I mean, family is family."

It took Doris June another moment to figure it all out. "Are you worried I'll miss my independence if I have to take care of you?"

"Oh, no." Mrs. Hargrove looked horrified.

"Well, I wouldn't, you know. You're my mother and it's only natural that I take care of you. I don't want you to feel you'd be imposing or limiting my independence."

"Oh, I wouldn't, I mean—" Mrs. Hargrove sputtered.

Doris June put her hand over her mother's hand. "I just want to be sure that you're not worried about anything. I'm here for you."

Mrs. Hargrove nodded. She looked as if she didn't know what to say. Finally, she lifted the plate of cookies. "Want another one?"

"Thanks," Doris June said as she took one. "I think I'll go up and look through the clothes in my old dresser. There has to be one of my old sweaters in there."

There was a moment's pause as Doris June looked at her mother to be sure she was okay.

Mrs. Hargrove swallowed. "Pick a pink one. You always look good in pink."

"I don't need to look good," Doris June said as she stood up. "I need to look authentic. If Curt and I dress up, we'll really just be playing a part. Almost like those living history exhibits, except we won't be that old."

"Whatever you say, dear," Mrs. Hargrove said as Doris June walked out of the kitchen.

Mrs. Hargrove hoped that Charley had been able to get more information out of Curt than she had been able to get out of Doris June, but she doubted it.

CHAPTER FOURTEEN

IT WAS AARON'S idea to honk the horn on the old pickup to announce that the concert was ready to begin. Linda had already made Aaron promise not to send any news releases to the local media. He assured her that he'd told the publicist for the Jazz Man to disregard his request. Then Aaron had promised Doris June that he wouldn't mention her in any follow-up news releases he sent out later. Both women thanked him.

"He should run for public office someday though," Linda said ruefully as she gave Doris June a stack of flyers to pass out to the teenagers who were still coming. "That guy could convince someone to thank him for stealing their purse because their hands got tired from holding it. He's always got an angle."

"Yeah, but look at all the trouble he's going to for the kids."

The evening air was cool and the gray of dusk was deepening into the dark of a full night. About a hundred teenagers were sitting around in the grass. Some of them had lawn chairs. Some of them were sitting on beach towels. All of them were holding a bright orange paper ensuring that, if they stayed for the talking part of the concert, they would get school credit for coming to the whole event. They had a generator, and the parking lights from several pickups were on to provide enough light so people didn't trip over any electrical cords as they found a place on the ground to sit.

Doris June had worn one of her old sweaters to the concert, but she had been chilly until Curt had draped his old letterman jacket over her shoulders. He had walked away before she could protest and, now that the sun had gone down completely, she was glad for the jacket's warmth.

"I recognize about thirty faces," Linda said to Doris June as she looked out over the teenagers. "That's about what Ben and Lucy expected from their friends around here. The other seventy are all bonus customers that Aaron brought in."

Ben and Lucy had decided to charge five dollars for the concert.

"And we're opening the café afterward," Linda said. "Lucy's hoping for a run on pie. We've got blueberry, peach and dark walnut."

The teenagers started to clap their hands as Aaron held up the microphone.

"Thanks for coming." Aaron brought the microphone down and shouted into it as a drumroll sounded from some electrical equipment Lucy had borrowed from the high school. "It's now my pleasure to bring you the one-and-only, the up-and-coming Bent Heart Band from downtown Dry Creek, Montana."

Ben and Lucy climbed up onto the back of the pickup amid the sound of cheers and began to sing.

Doris June felt herself start to relax. The concert had begun and no one had pointed a finger at her and demanded to know what had happened that night when the sign got crumpled into its current shape. She glanced over at the thing. It was still just a rusted old sign, but it looked different tonight. Several candles in tall jars were burning at the bottom of the stop sign and someone had placed a cellophane-wrapped bouquet of roses next to the candles.

"It looks like an altar," Doris June muttered to Linda as they stood at the back of the teenagers.

"Or one of those places where there's been a shooting. You know, the ones that get on television because there's some scandal involved."

"Hey, there's no scandal here."

Linda grinned. "The night is young."

Doris June just chuckled. She was beginning to feel a little more comfortable about the whole concert. She knew that teenagers in a rural area often had to make their own entertainment. All this was, really, was a big party.

Ben and Lucy finished their first song and the audience clapped with enthusiasm.

Ben pulled the microphone closer. "Before we get any further along, Aaron is going to introduce the two people who made this all possible—the original Bent Heart Pair—"

It took Doris June a second to realize Ben was referring to her and Curt. By then, it was too late to hide because Ben had already passed the microphone down to Aaron and they were both motioning for her and Curt to come forward.

"Let's give them a hand," Aaron shouted into his microphone as the teenagers started standing up and stomping as they clapped and yelled. "These are the two people who were kissing so hard they hit a stop sign and made history."

"I don't think you have a choice," Linda whispered to Doris June.

Doris June had already recognized that fact so she put a cheerful smile on her face. She'd agreed to talk to the teenagers tonight; she might as well have an introduction.

Doris June hugged the jacket a little closer as she walked to the front of the crowd. The jacket was big enough she could almost hide inside it. She remembered that feeling from when she wore it in high school. She had never felt safer than the times when she had been in Curt's jacket. It smelled like him, too, which was nice.

When she reached Aaron, Doris June stopped and turned around. Curt had walked over from another direction and they were each standing on opposite sides of Aaron.

"Well, we can't have this," Aaron said as he looked at Doris June and then turned his head to look at Curt. "I'm not going to be the one who comes between this teenage couple."

Aaron took an exaggerated step back and motioned Doris June and Curt to close ranks so they would be standing next to each other.

Doris June figured she had agreed to be a good sport when she'd said she would talk to the students. She did hope, however, that Aaron would get to the serious part of things before too long. He probably felt he had to draw things out to make them more dramatic, she decided, as she took a small step closer to Curt. That was entertainment these days.

"There you have it," Aaron announced. "The original eloping couple."

The kids went wild with their clapping.

Aaron encouraged them. "The couple that didn't get away."

Doris June forced herself to keep smiling. The man couldn't keep going on much longer. At least, she hoped not.

"I give you our very own Doris June Hargrove and Curt Nelson," Aaron shouted.

The clapping got even more frantic.

Finally, Aaron stepped closer and whispered to Doris June and Curt. "Can't you two look a little more friendly?"

Aaron kept the microphone covered so the crowd fortunately couldn't hear his words.

"We're friendly," Doris June snapped back in a low voice.

"You're still standing miles apart," Aaron protested quietly. "You're supposed to be in love."

"That was twenty-five years ago," Doris June hissed back at him.

Curt took a big step closer to Doris June so that they were standing beside each other.

It wasn't enough. The crowd had stopped clapping and was now stamping their feet on the ground. Doris June worried that the vibrations of all of that stamping might upset the candles by the stop sign and ignite a fire. She burrowed a little further into Curt's jacket. She certainly hadn't been this timid in high school. The girl who used to wear this jacket wouldn't stand here letting a crowd build up steam like this. She knew what they wanted. Some kids were bold enough to call out their demand for a kiss.

"Oh, this is ridiculous," Doris June finally said. There was no point in continuing to make a spectacle of themselves and she could see from the cautious light in Curt's eyes that he wasn't going to do anything to stop all this noise.

Doris June was a businesswoman. She knew that the best way to move a meeting along was to finish up the one topic everyone had on their minds so they could concentrate on everything else. She took a deep breath and inhaled the scent of the jacket.

Then she did what everyone wanted. She reached up and pulled Curt's head down and gave him the same kind of kiss she'd given him twenty-five years ago in almost this same spot.

Oh. Doris June was stunned. Not just because of the kiss, as good as that was. Curt had always been a good kisser. That hadn't changed. Well, maybe it had a little. Her heart couldn't take much more of this. She heard pounding and Lucy hadn't turned on the drum machine. Oh, my.

Doris June forced herself to think. It wasn't just this kiss. She was suddenly remembering what had happened twenty-five years ago on this spot. She'd reached up and grabbed Curt just like she'd done now.

Only, he'd been driving the pickup back then. Which meant she was the one who had caused them to run into the stop sign. It had all been her fault.

Doris June was out of breath when the kiss ended. Part of that was because of

Curt, of course. She was relieved to see that he looked as shaken by the whole thing as she felt. But that wasn't all of it. She was horrified because she realized for the first time that she'd been blaming Curt for something for years and she had been the one who was responsible all along.

"Wow," Curt said softly.

Doris June nodded. That was all she could do.

The cheering had reached its peak with the kiss and the teenagers were quieting down now that they had what they wanted. Doris June started to walk away from the front stage area while Aaron was introducing the next song Ben and Lucy were going to play.

"Easy," Curt said as he reached out to steady her. "Electrical cord there."

Doris June only nodded. She let him lead her away.

They were at the back of the audience again before Doris June found her voice. She looked up at Curt, the man whose jacket she still wore. "I'm so sorry."

"Don't mention it," Curt said as his jaw

tightened. "We were just doing what we had to do."

"No, I—" Doris June began again, but suddenly she was talking to empty air. Curt had stepped away.

Linda moved closer to her. "Are you okay? I could get us some chairs."

Doris June shook her head. "No, I'm fine. I just realized what a fool I've been."

The air was filled with the sound of more cheers as Ben and Lucy finished another song.

Linda nodded in sympathy. "We've all been there. We look at the man we thought we loved and realize it's all smoke and mirrors. That's what it's been for years, of course, we just didn't see it. Or didn't want to see it."

"Oh, no, it's not Curt," Doris June said, as she decided maybe she would sit down after all. She slowly lowered herself to the ground and sat cross-legged. "It's me."

Linda sat down next to Doris June and looked at her curiously. The song that Ben and Lucy were singing now required audience participation, however, and it was much too loud to talk so both women joined in the singing instead.

Which was just as well, Doris June told herself. She needed to do some thinking before she even knew what to say about all of this. How could she have been wrong all this time? If Curt hadn't been to blame for that day, what sense did any of it make? She'd spent years of her life thinking their botched elopement was his fault. Oh, maybe not every day. She'd hardly even thought about how wrong their lives had gone these past few years until her mother called and asked her to come back to help with the Mother's Day baskets. But even when she'd stopped thinking about Curt, she'd let that day influence her outlook on life.

The stop sign was such a small thing to have had such a big impact in her life.

Doris June didn't know how she could have been such a fool as to not see that she had been the one who caused them to hit the stop sign. There was enough light from the pickups that she could see Curt now. He was standing over where Charley and her mother were sitting on a couple of folding chairs. She could see him talking to them and he seemed to be doing fine.

Doris June wondered if Curt had figured out that she was the one to blame for them hitting the stop sign. Of course he had, she told herself. He'd probably figured it out that day in the sheriff's office. Curt had never said anything to the sheriff about the kiss. He'd just said he wasn't paying enough attention to the road. The fact that he hadn't mentioned it didn't mean he didn't know it had happened, though.

It isn't often, Doris June told herself, that her world tilted on its axis. She was used to knowing what had happened, when it had happened and why it had happened. She wasn't the kind of person who suddenly realized the past hadn't been as she remembered it.

She looked at Curt again. Why hadn't he told her? That's what a friend would do. A friend told you if you had broccoli in your teeth. No wonder he looked like he was waiting for her to say something more each time he'd apologized. He probably thought she was in complete denial.

She cuddled a little deeper into the jacket Curt had given her to wear. Why weren't things as simple as they used to be? She kept watching Curt as he started walking around at the edge of the concert. At first, she thought he was going to walk back to where she was. But he didn't. He looked as if he was making his way back to their parents. Not that it mattered. When the intermission came, she was going to find him no matter where he was in the crowd and tell him how very sorry she was that she had blamed him all those years ago. And, then she was going to say that she'd like to be friends again.

He'd asked to be friends again and she'd thought at the time that he might have something more romantic in mind. Well, if he did, she was going to say yes. She missed Curt now and had for years.

When the clapping died down from the next song, Aaron informed everyone that they were going to hear from another generation in the Bent Heart story.

"Let's welcome Mrs. Hargrove and Charley Nelson," Aaron announced into his microphone.

Doris June was glad to see that Curt was there to help her mother up from the folding chair and to hold her arm as they walked over to the front of the concert. Even though her mother didn't need that kind of help during the day, Doris June knew her mother didn't see so well at night any longer.

The teenagers clapped just as hard for her mother and Charley as they had for Curt and herself. They really were good kids, Doris June thought to herself. She was glad she and Curt had said it was okay to use the old sign for the concert.

Mrs. Hargrove waited for the cheering to die down and then she started to say something. No one could hear what it was she was saying, but Aaron moved his microphone over to her.

Her words started to get louder in the middle of her sentence. "...why it's important to give your parents their respect. They don't always know what is best to do and they need your understanding."

"Are you saying you regret tearing your daughter and Curt Nelson apart all of those years ago?" Aaron swung the microphone toward him and asked his question as if he was Anderson Cooper or somebody.

Aaron moved the microphone back quickly so everyone would catch Mrs. Hargrove's answer. "Well, seventeen is too young to get married. We all know that." There was a groan in the audience, but that didn't stop Mrs. Hargrove. She just looked out at the teenagers. "You know that's true, Tommy McLain, so don't go thinking about it. No, what I am saying is that I regret the way I did it. Maybe if I had done things differently, it would have been better. I mean, I haven't even told Curt Nelson how sorry I am for the way I treated him back then."

Mrs. Hargrove stopped to look over at Curt, which was easy enough to do since he was standing right next to her still holding her arm in case she got unsteady on her feet.

Aaron leaned over so he could speak into

the microphone. "And how does Curt feel about that?"

Aaron held the microphone up higher and angled it so it was even with Curt's chin. "I don't—"

There was silence for a minute.

"Come on, Curt," Aaron said into the microphone. "We're all here to learn about how families can relate better. Don't be shy. What do you think of Mrs. Hargrove's apology?"

Curt reached out and took the microphone from Aaron. "First off, she doesn't need to apologize to me. I've thought about it lately, and she did the exact right thing."

"I did?" Mrs. Hargrove asked, and even without a microphone Doris June could hear the surprise in her mother's voice.

"Absolutely," Curt answered. His words were strong and he had no hesitation. "You knew what needed to be done and you did it. I owe you my thanks."

With that, Curt kissed Mrs. Hargrove on the cheek and the teenagers went wild again. Doris June was glad for all the noise. She was sure no one had heard the quick gasp she'd made when Curt said her mother was right about tearing them apart. She thought he had at least grieved over their shattered plans. But it didn't appear that he had. The thought had never occurred to Doris June that maybe Curt had wanted someone to stop them from eloping.

She pulled the jacket closer around her, but, for the first time that evening, it didn't make her warmer. She was so cold she thought she must be coming down with something; maybe it was the flu, because she felt aches all over.

The next song Ben and Lucy played was a slow love ballad that was very sad. No one would think it strange to see a woman shedding a tear or two while she listened to it, Doris June told herself. Lots of people cried a little at sad love songs.

CHAPTER FIFTEEN

THE AIR GREW cooler as the evening progressed and started to become moist. It was almost as if the night dew was already coming. If the teenagers noticed, they just huddled closer together. Doris June walked up to Aaron in the intermission and told him she was a little tired. He assured her it was fine if she didn't talk any more for the rest of the program.

"You've already given us a good segment," he said as he held a camera in his hand. He was taking publicity shots. "Besides, your mother has those kids in the palm of her hand. She's an educational phenomenon. We need to get her in the classrooms."

Doris June nodded.

Mrs. Hargrove had done a particularly fine segment, Doris June thought, on how teenagers could improve their relationships with their parents in the good times so they could handle the bad times together better. This was after Curt's remarks and before Aaron called for the intermission.

At the beginning of intermission, Linda and Curt passed around big plastic tubs of cookies. There were chocolate-chip cookies in one and oatmeal cookies in the other. Linda also had a tub of plastic-wrapped chocolate doughnuts that she set beside the stop sign and invited everyone to share.

After they ate their cookies, some of the teenagers gathered around the old pickup and Ben started telling them all about the wild drive that night long ago and how the pickup had hit the stop sign and bent it until it became the shape that it is today. He used motions and sound effects and, Doris June decided, his version was even more exciting than the real thing.

She didn't listen to the full story, however. Her attention strayed to a boy and girl over at the stop sign who were kneeling down and looking for a place to carve their initials. She supposed it was a violation of some sort to deface public property, but she doubted that knowledge would stop anyone here tonight.

"Hey, is this *them?*" the boy suddenly shouted from where he was kneeling. "Look at this, it says 'D.J.H. + C.N.' That's got to be Doris June Hargrove loves Curt Nelson. The letters are all rusted out, but you can see them if you get close."

Doris June was glad that it was nighttime and no one could see reddened faces even if they did get close.

Ben left the side of the pickup and walked over to the stop sign. He bent down and then stood back up and looked for Curt. "Way to go, Dad! I bet you were the first one to even scratch anything on the old post."

Ben gave his father a grin and a thumbs-up sign.

Curt nodded back at his son. Of course, he couldn't do much else because he was holding the plastic tub of cookies with both hands. Doris June hoped Curt believed the kids were seeing things. Those scratchy letters had to be so rusted that they could spell anything. He didn't rush over to check the letters so he must know that everyone could be mistaken.

Doris June decided she should go back to the shadows and sit down before anything else embarrassing happened. No sooner had she done that than Aaron declared the intermission over. Doris June never thought she would be so glad to have a band start playing again.

The first song after the break was an upbeat song Lucy had written about finding love in unexpected people.

"They each wrote a song," Linda whispered as she sat down next to Doris June in the area they'd shared during the first part of the concert. Linda had the plastic tub, now empty of cookies, and she set it down in front of them so they could lean their elbows on it as they sat cross-legged.

"It's a good song," Doris June answered softly as Lucy drew the words to a close. "It's got a tune you can hum."

"You don't think I should worry, do you?" Linda asked, keeping her voice low. "She's kind of young for a steady boyfriend."

Doris June smiled. "Just because she puts words to a song it doesn't mean she has anyone particular in mind. You don't know that she's really found anything."

Linda nodded. "I suppose it could be creative license. It's just I worry about her since our mother is gone."

"She's got you."

"I guess. It's just that I've never been much good when it comes to understanding men," Linda said. "Not like a mother would be."

"I don't think it's so easy to be a mother even if it's your daughter and not your little sister."

"Yeah, I suppose not."

"If you really run into problems, talk to my mother," Doris June suggested. "She's good at this parenting stuff."

"I'll do that."

Ben was now kneeling down at the front of the stage and holding the microphone. "Before I sing the song I wrote, I want Mrs. Hargrove to step up close to the pickup here."

Doris June watched as Curt escorted her

mother up to the front again. He really was such a nice man, she thought. In the light coming from the other pickups, she could see he was relaxed and friendly to everyone. He was smiling and having a good time. Of course, she reminded herself, he hadn't had a shock earlier in the evening and realized that he was the one responsible for something he'd always blamed on someone else. Guilt could dampen anyone's enthusiasm.

When Mrs. Hargrove was settled next to the bed of the pickup, Ben started to talk.

"I don't remember my mother," Ben said. "But I can remember, even before I moved to Dry Creek, that Mrs. Hargrove always took time to ask me how I was and to bring me some cookies if she knew I was in town visiting my grandfather. So, since it's Mother's Day tomorrow, I want to dedicate this song to her."

Ben's song was about moving from the city streets of Chicago to the old roads of Dry Creek and how he'd found a home on the roads that he couldn't find on the city streets. It was because of neighbors, the last line of his song went—it was all because of the neighbors who shared those old country roads with him.

Mrs. Hargrove gave Ben a hug when he'd finished his song and leaned into the microphone. "I'm going to ask him to sing that song in the town hall tomorrow so come on over and hear it again."

Lucy leaned into the microphone, too. "And we wanted everyone to know that the town is making Mother's Day baskets for everyone's mothers so if you want to help with the bows, meet us after the concert. Everyone's welcome to help, even if you don't have a mother of your own."

"Those who have more mother than they need have offered to share with us," Ben said, and everyone laughed.

The next several songs had strong rhythms and were ones everyone knew so some of the teenagers stood up and sang along, swaying to the beat. Doris June was glad the concert was almost over.

"So, are you okay?" Linda asked. The

final song was fading away and everyone else was getting up.

"I'll be fine," Doris June said. "I just—well, it's been quite a day."

Linda nodded. "Okay, then."

Doris June stood up and stretched. She wondered at what point tonight she was supposed to give the jacket back to Curt. She knew she needed to talk to him; she was just hoping to avoid it until she'd had a full night's rest. She didn't want to say one wrong word to Curt. If there was still a chance that they could be friends again, she wanted to be careful and not damage it.

After Charley had led a group of teenagers over to the town hall to tie bows on baskets and Curt had started off with his son taking the equipment they'd borrowed into the café, Doris June walked over to her mother and gave her a hug.

"Did you see that?" Mrs. Hargrove asked in delight. "I was sung to by Ben. He remembered those cookies I used to give him."

Doris June smiled. "I saw. It was great."

"This concert was a wonderful idea."

Doris June nodded. It had certainly been educational.

Mrs. Hargrove leaned in close to Doris June. "And I invited Aaron to stay in my hotel room tonight and come to the celebration with us tomorrow. He said he might be able to get my room in some travel road guides as a bed-and-breakfast."

"He'd be the one to do it, all right."

Doris June walked her mother back to her house and they talked about sheets.

"I have the yellow plaid ones I could use on that bed up there," Mrs. Hargrove said as she carefully stepped over a rut in the road. "But I don't want him to think the place is not sophisticated. I also have a couple of pink sheets, but that doesn't seem very manly. That would be more for couples, don't you think?"

Mrs. Hargrove turned to Doris June.

"I think either set of sheets will be just fine. Or you can tell him that you have options and that you pick the sheets based on your impressions of the guest."

"Oh, that's perfect," Mrs. Hargrove said.

"Aaron will like that. He can use it as an angle."

"I think the breakfast you make for the person in the morning will be your best sales point." Doris June frowned. She wasn't so sure it was safe for her mother to take strangers into her dining room. "You do call Charley when there's someone staying over, don't you? Or, the sheriff or someone."

Mrs. Hargrove nodded. "You know Charley. He insists on having breakfast with us when I have a paying guest."

"Well, that's a good thing. I'm glad to see Charley worries about you, too."

Mrs. Hargrove grunted. "I don't know how worried he is. He gets a free breakfast. Besides, he's usually just sitting over in the hardware store in the morning anyway so it's good exercise for him to walk over."

"Well, he won't have to come tomorrow morning, since I will be here."

"With a late time tonight, I think he'll appreciate that."

Doris June offered to get the room ready for Aaron. She changed the sheets, so he could sleep on the yellow plaid ones instead of the pink ones. She plugged the television in so he could watch the news in the morning.

Ordinarily, she would adjust the antenna on the roof so he'd get a little better picture reception, but since it was night, Doris June decided Aaron could close his eyes if he needed to and imagine the news pictures. The sound of the announcers came in clear and that would have to be enough.

When Doris June went back into her mother's house, she smelled cinnamon. She went into the kitchen. Her mother was getting ingredients ready for breakfast.

"I hope he likes sweet rolls. I'm taking some out of the freezer so they'll be ready to bake in the morning. And I'm going to have cooked oatmeal with cinnamon and maybe my own sugared chokecherries. I would do French toast, but I want to leave us lots of time to get ready for the celebration."

"It sounds perfect," Doris June said as she kissed her mother on the cheek. "I'll see you in the morning. Don't stay up late."

"I'm right behind you."

Doris June never remembered her bed feeling so good. She used to like to lie in bed at night and think about the day. Sometimes she could get up and go sit at her window and think. With the lights off in her room, she could look out of the second-floor window and see the stars. After Doris June heard her mother climb the stairs, she got out of bed and went and sat by her window.

Doris June saw a light go on in the room over the garage. Her mother's guest was home. She hoped he liked his yellow plaid sheets. Quietly, she moved her chair a little to the right so she could see most of the road going through Dry Creek. There were a few black shapes where vehicles were still parked on the side of the road and a nightlight in the parsonage next to the church. The one streetlight was farther down so Doris June didn't see the light pole even though she saw the circle of fuzzy light it gave off.

She wondered if Curt would ask for his jacket back tomorrow. She'd forgotten about it in her decision to walk her mother home in the darkness. Doris June turned around to where the jacket hung on a hook behind her door. She was a little chilled, she thought, as she stood up and walked over to the door to get the jacket. Once she had it on, she snuggled down in it.

CHAPTER SIXTEEN

DORIS JUNE THOUGHT she smelled pansies before she even opened the door to the town hall the next morning, but maybe it was the smell of the dirt around the pansies. Whatever it was, she took a deep breath. Aaron was walking beside her; her mother and Charley were walking together behind them. Even though Charley hadn't come for breakfast, he had stopped by so that he could walk her mother to the celebration, which Doris June thought was kind of sweet.

Of course, Charley did admit he had enough of an appetite to eat one of Mrs. Hargrove's cinnamon rolls even though he'd already had breakfast at home. The fact that Charley had organized the teenagers last night so well that Mrs. Hargrove didn't have to go in early and finish getting the baskets ready made her more than willing to feed him.

Doris June looked behind her just to be sure her mother and Charley had both made it up the stairs fine.

"You know, really, your mother needs to patent that recipe she uses to make her cooked oatmeal," Aaron mumbled for the third time as he followed Doris June down one of the aisles. "There are people out there who will try to steal it from her if they get a chance. I've never tasted anything like those sugared chokecherries she puts in it. She could make a fortune with them alone."

"I don't think that she wants a fortune," Doris June whispered.

Aaron's eyes went big at that and then he nodded, understanding.

Doris June sat down in a chair and laid Curt's jacket out to the right of her. Her mind this morning was a mess and it was all over something as humble as a jacket. She knew she needed to return Curt's jacket, but she didn't want to be wearing it when she had to do that. It would be hard enough giving it back; she didn't want to have the memory of Curt taking if off her shoulders as well. Plus, she needed to find a way to apologize to him and that wasn't going to be easy.

Doris June knew the minute Curt and Ben entered the town hall.

As the mayor began to speak, Doris June wondered if other people were having as hard a time concentrating as she was because of all of the beauty in the front of the hall. A tower of pansy baskets filled the front wall with all different colors of bows poking out between the flowers and the leaves.

Mrs. Hargrove and Charley both joined the mayor up at the front when it was time to begin handing out the pansy baskets. They each had some white cards in their hands which looked like speech notes, but the first thing Mrs. Hargrove asked was for Ben to come forward to sing his song and she didn't use notes for that.

No one made a sound as Ben played the guitar and sang his song about the country roads of Dry Creek and how they welcomed him home every time he walked them. Doris June almost cried. She knew just how he felt. She was missing those roads, too, and the people who lived beside them.

Instead of having the mothers all stand this year and just passing the pansies down the rows until each got one, Charley announced that some helpers were going to personally deliver the pansies this year. Most of the local teens who had been at the concert last night were there, and they went to the front of the hall. Each teen took a basket from Charley and got whispered instructions from him based on his checklist. The teenagers took baskets to their own mothers first and delivered them with a kiss on their mothers' cheeks.

About that time, Doris June realized she wasn't the only one with tears in her eyes. Of course, with some of the mothers, it might have been tears from the shock at seeing their teenage sons doing something as sentimental as passing out flowers. The kids kept at it until every mother had a basket overflowing with pansies.

And then Ben stood at the pulpit again. "We have a couple of special presentations to people who mean a lot to us, but who aren't mothers."

Ben then took two baskets from the front and walked down the aisle until he reached the aisle where Doris June sat.

"First, this one is for Aaron," Ben said as he held out a basket to the man. "Because he worried over us more than any mother would when we had our concert last night and we owe him for that."

Aaron chuckled as he reached out for the basket. "I'll remember this."

Doris June wasn't sure if that was a promise or a threat or both. Ben just laughed it off.

"And the other one is for Doris June," Ben said as he held out a basket. He looked a little shy, but he kept going. "We want her to know we appreciate her letting us go forward with the concert even though it meant she had to kiss my dad."

A ripple of chuckles greeted this.

Doris June took the basket anyway. "I'll remember, too."

Ben blushed a little at that.

"Me, too," he said, and unlike Aaron's earlier words, it didn't sound like a threat.

Once everyone had their baskets, the noise level rose as everyone remarked on the velvet colors of the pansies and the shiny brightness of the bows and how beautiful the baskets were and what a wonderful Mother's Day it was.

"I should have had a picture," Aaron said as he looked around at the baskets in excitement. "I left my camera in my suitcase. Doesn't somebody have a camera?"

Aaron muttered something to Doris June about seeing the strap of a camera bag on someone's shoulder and he was off to see if he could persuade his target to take a picture of some of the baskets.

Doris June saw her mother walking over to her and she sat back down.

"Happy Mother's Day," Doris June said to Mrs. Hargrove as her mother came and sat beside her.

"It's been one of the best," Mrs. Hargrove said with shining eyes. "Did you see? All of those young people came by and gave me a kiss when they were passing out their baskets. They didn't have to—I wasn't even the one they were giving their baskets to."

"I think you're a mother to more children around here than you realize."

"I used to feel bad that I wasn't a grandmother," Mrs. Hargrove admitted sheepishly. "I never realized I have all the grandchildren a woman could ever love."

Doris June smiled. "Certainly all she could ever feed."

Mrs. Hargrove arched an eyebrow. "That's not to say I couldn't love more children if you were to—"

Doris June shook her head. "You're incorrigible."

"I'm just saying if," Mrs. Hargrove said. "There's nothing wrong with dreaming."

The crowd in the town hall had begun so spill out into the square so Mrs. Hargrove stood up and went to the front to begin straightening up things. She left her pansy basket on the pew.

Doris June kept hoping there would be some reason to put off returning Curt's jacket, but he seemed to be waiting around just as she was, so finally she picked the jacket up and crossed to where he still sat.

"I wanted to thank you for lending me this last night," Doris June said as she held out the jacket. "I should have known it would get cold enough to need a jacket."

Curt stood up. "That old jacket takes you back, doesn't it?"

Doris June smiled. "It sure does. Thanks again for letting me wear it."

Curt still didn't take the jacket, even though she was holding it out to him. Finally, he cleared his throat. "I was kind of hoping you'd like to keep it for a while."

"Really? I mean, I have a jacket at Mom's. I just wasn't wearing it last night."

"Well, yes, but that one at your mom's is not *my* jacket," Curt said softly. "I was hoping you would wear my jacket."

Doris June looked up at him. "What?"

"I figure that's where we went wrong. I should have asked you to be my steady girlfriend instead of my wife. So, I'm asking you to wear my jacket. I would have asked you to wear my class ring, but I couldn't find it."

"You went looking for your class ring?"

"I thought it was in my sock drawer, but it's not."

"But why?" Doris June frowned.

"I figure I pushed you to be something you weren't ready to be back then."

"That's not true. I wanted to be—"

Curt put his fingers on her lips. "It's okay. It was my fault."

"No, it wasn't," Doris June whispered. "I realized last night that it was all my fault. I'm the one who made us crash into the stop sign. I'm the one who said we had to report it to the sheriff. I'm the one who got our parents involved."

Curt opened his arms to her at this and she leaned into them. The jacket fell to the row of chairs between them. He smoothed back her hair. "It's okay, I knew you did those things so you wouldn't have to go to Las Vegas with me."

"You knew?" Doris June lifted her head off his chest so she could look him in the eye.

Curt nodded. "I thought you knew, too. I thought I'd scared you away for good."

Doris June shook her head. "I swear I didn't know. I just thought things were happening and then you ran out of the sheriff's office and left and— You knew then, didn't you?"

Curt nodded. "I wasn't mad at the sheriff. I thought you weren't interested in me. Not like I was interested in you."

"But how could you *think* that?"

Curt's shoulder shielded her from a sudden flash, but Doris June knew what it meant anyway. She looked around Curt's shoulder and saw Aaron taking their picture.

"We don't have anything to do with Mother's Day," Doris June snapped at Aaron. "So you don't need a picture of us."

Aaron shrugged. "I'm just surprised you can do things like that in public. Kissing and all."

"We weren't kissing," Doris June said.

"Well, give me some time here." Curt grinned. "I'm getting around to it."

Curt looked over Doris June's head and straight at Aaron. "Just so you know, people kiss all of the time in public here."

"Well, maybe in weddings," Aaron conceded. "And like today, but that's kids kissing their mothers. And I suppose—"

Aaron stopped when he realized no one was listening to him. Curt was kissing Doris June. Aaron looked around and noticed that two other people seemed as interested in the kiss going on as he was. Mrs. Hargrove and Charley had both stopped and were standing there smiling at their children.

Since no one was watching him anymore, Aaron decided to take one more quick picture. He figured Ben might like it if he put together one of those history videos for his dad's wedding reception. Of course, Aaron was just speculating about the wedding. But then, he told himself as he turned and walked back down the aisle, he was very good at speculation.

IT WAS THE next Wednesday night before the Nelsons came to the Hargroves' for dinner again. This time they had lasagna with garlic bread. It was almost eight o'clock and Mrs. Hargrove and Charley were in the kitchen. They had finished doing the dishes and were sitting at a small table by the back door trying not to strain to hear what was being said in the living room. Which, as they both knew, wasn't that easy to do even though they had purposely left the dining room empty between the kitchen and the living room just so anyone in the living room would know they had privacy.

"Too bad we finished that state form," Mrs. Hargrove finally said just for something to say. She and Charley had mailed their form to Aaron yesterday. It had been much easier to write once Doris June and Curt were both happy to have the stop sign be the center of attention.

Charley grunted. "With all the worrying we did beforehand, we spent enough time on it."

Mrs. Hargrove nodded. "Worry isn't always bad, though."

They sat together for a few more minutes.

"I wonder how Ben is doing over at the café," Charley finally asked. He kept wondering if it would hurt to sneak into the dining room. Maybe he could hear something of what was going on.

"Ben and Lucy have counted their money so many times already, I don't know why they bother," Mrs. Hargrove said.

"Well, it gives them something to do where they can be together."

"At least Linda's there to chaperone them." Mrs. Hargrove found that, ever since Ben had said such nice things about her, she was starting to fret over him just like a grandmother would.

"Which leaves us to chaperone—" Charley lifted his eyebrow and glanced in the direction of the living room. He didn't need to say anything more. "Not that they need a chaperone."

"Doris June will always be my baby."

"It's taken them a long time to get together."

"Love requires patience," Mrs. Hargrove said.

Charley blushed at that, although he consoled himself with the thought that his face was weathered enough that no one would notice. He had already figured out that love required patience. He had decided to take a clue from his son's disastrous first courtship with Doris June and to be patient. The Hargrove women had to make their own decisions about when they were ready for romance and he wasn't going to push Edith on the subject.

"I thought they'd at least have come out for a second helping of your pineapple upside-down cake," Charley finally said.

"Would you like more?"

"Don't mind if I do," Charley said. He wouldn't lose any weight by being patient, that was for sure. Lasagna might be Curt's favorite, but the pineapple upside-down cake was for him.

Mrs. Hargrove dished up another serving of dessert for Charley and watched him eat it. Then she put the bowl in the sink and looked at the clock. It had all only taken fifteen minutes.

"Well, I can't stand it," Mrs. Hargrove finally announced as she stood up and walked into the dining room. From there she could see through the doorway into the living room. She frowned at what she saw.

The ceiling light was shining brightly and no one had even bothered to close the door between the dining room and the living room.

Mrs. Hargrove had vowed to not interfere in her daughter's love life again, but sometimes a mother's hand was needed. She didn't even have to look into the living room. All she needed to do was slip her hand around the doorjamb so she could flip off the overhead light and shut the door.

Doris June and Curt were sitting on the sofa in the living room. They had sneaked out of the house for a quick evening walk down to their sign and they had just sat back down again when the living room was plunged into darkness.

"Is something wrong with a fuse?" Doris June asked, until she saw that the small table lamp in the corner was still on.

Curt shook his head. "I saw a hand reach in and switch the light off. And close the door, too."

Doris June nodded as she settled back into the curve of Curt's arm. "My mother."

"I guess she approves."

"Well, we did miss out on a lot of dates," Doris June said. "She's just moving us along."

"Hey, I'm not rushing any of those dates," Curt said as he bent down to kiss Doris June fully on the lips. "What year are we working on by now anyway?"

"We're up to 1995," Doris June said.

"Ah," Curt said as he bent to kiss her again. "That's a good year."

"They're all good years," Doris June said as she leaned in for another kiss.

* * * * *